The Kingdom of Zynthia: Bloodline

Jeremy Gillespie

TRILOGY CHRISTIAN PUBLISHERS
Tustin, CA

Trilogy Christian Publishers

A Wholly Owned Subsidiary of Trinity Broadcasting Network

2442 Michelle Drive

Tustin, CA 92780

The Kingdom of Zynthia: Bloodline

Copyright © 2024 by Jeremy Gillespie

All rights reserved, including the right to reproduce this book or portions thereof in any form whatsoever.

For information, address Trilogy Christian Publishing

Rights Department, 2442 Michelle Drive, Tustin, Ca 92780.

Trilogy Christian Publishing/TBN and colophon are trademarks of Trinity Broadcasting Network.

For information about special discounts for bulk purchases, please contact Trilogy Christian Publishing.

Trilogy Disclaimer: The views and content expressed in this book are those of the author and may not necessarily reflect the views and doctrine of Trilogy Christian Publishing or the Trinity Broadcasting Network.

10 9 8 7 6 5 4 3 2 1

Library of Congress Cataloging-in-Publication Data is available.

ISBN 979-8-89333-323-7

ISBN 979-8-89333-324-4 (ebook)

Contents

Chapter 1. A Family of Unicorns 1

Chapter 2. Troubled Travels 19

Chapter 3. Welcome Home, in a Court Room 39

Chapter 4. An Unwanted Dream 58

Chapter 5. The Path to the Truth 79

Chapter 6. Trouble Found Us 93

Chapter 7. Secrets Uncovered 114

Chapter 8. The Cloak of Light 127

Chapter 9. Battle for Eru Psyawla 144

Chapter 10. Welcome Back with a Surprise 161

Chapter 11. Battle Number Two 177

Chapter 12. A Field of Dead Flowers 191

Chapter 13. New Beginnings 209

CHAPTER 1

A Family of Unicorns

I trudged home through the darkening forest, disappointed that my efforts were unsuccessful for the third time this week. As I gazed out into the horizon, my eyes drifted to a family of unicorns drinking from the river. The sun shining through the trees cast a golden aura around them, adding a sense of ethereal beauty to the already rare scene. I followed this river home every time I ventured out into the Woodlands, yet never had I witnessed a scene so magical and so majestic as the one before me now. *Maybe if it were just one, it wouldn't be a big deal, but four!* I thought in awe. I hitched my bow higher on my back as I continued to watch them. Hunting a unicorn is something elves just don't do. It's not illegal, but morally speaking, it would be a devastating and heinous crime. I wouldn't disgrace myself by killing a unicorn, no matter how frustrated I was about going home empty-handed.

"How beautiful! How graceful you creatures are," I whispered as I cautiously approached them. I shouldn't get too close. Wild unicorns frighten easily; they won't attack, but they will defend themselves if they perceive me as a threat. I stood for a moment a short distance away, nodded my head to show my respect, and then continued on my way.

As I emerged from the trees on the edge of VaHaile, a small village in the Kingdom of Zynthia, I sensed the overwhelming feeling of shame flowing from my peers as they saw me return having, yet again, not managed to bring home even so much as a slorg, the slow-moving and frankly dumb cousin of rabbits that inhabit the woods near our village. As an elf approaching twenty-three years of age, I should've found my place among my people by now. Hunting definitely wasn't one of my strengths. I was disastrous at steel and woodworking, these being how our weapons and buildings are made, not to mention the fires I caused during my rotations with those masters. Cooking, well, I could do enough to survive, but not many would want to buy the food I made or call them masterpieces. There are multiple jobs and duties that elves can master and *zero* in which I had excelled. At least so far. Some elves can possess gifts of different sorts. Rare, but it's true. Some control nature. Some can shape-shift. Even more rare are those who create blasts of explosive power; those usually become warriors in the High Elf Ranger Brigade. Though, you don't need these unique skills to become a Ranger. Regular elves can be one, too, and most of the Rangers are "normal."

"Torren, empty-handed again, I see," Miri laughed. Miri Masel, my best friend in the entire kingdom. I could trust her with anything, especially to give me a good laugh. She wore these very elegant tunics and dresses, usually embellished with green or pink that matched perfectly with her necklace, which alternated four pink and green stones and wrapped around with a white chain. She had deep brown hair, and her blue eyes seemed to change tinge based on the color of the sky. Her skin was soft as silk, but her hands were a bit rough, as she wasn't afraid of hard work; independence was important to her. Miri was beautiful in every way, inside and out.

"Ha, Miri. I tried," I sighed, "but it just wasn't my day, I guess."

"It seems that it's never your day, Torren," Miri retorted playfully. Miri had been my friend since we were little. She was also one of the elves who found her calling early on. She poked fun and picked at me, but all in love. I know she didn't mean any actual harm.

"Torren, what is your passion?" Miri asked.

"Mir, not now, please," I said as I set my bow and quiver of arrows on the table outside my house. Without another word, we gathered our packs, checking to be sure I had everything I needed, and we set off toward the village center together. As we walked through the village, I felt a sense of unease, as if someone was watching us just out of sight.

"Are you okay? You're zoning out again," Miri asked worriedly.

"Yeah, I'm fine. Just hungry," I said. "Let's see if Olive has any makian soup and fig cookies left," I suggested, hopefully. Makian soup consists of basil, makian stock, tender chunks of makian, cheese, leaves from a krunbal bush, and little pieces of egg. Though I felt certain that someone was out there, I didn't want to worry Miri with it for the time being. She would just say I was being stupid and paranoid, which I supposed was at least half true.

After we finished eating, Miri waved goodbye as she headed toward her house. I decided to go to my favorite spot just on the edge of town, along the tree line, where I felt free and safe. About midway up a hawthorn tree was a fork so comfortable it seemed to have been crafted just for me. It was peaceful high in the quiet treetops. I could have easily fallen asleep if it weren't for the return of that nagging feeling of eyes watching me. I frantically searched the area from my vantage point high in the tree. Finding no one and no impending danger, I climbed down and quietly set off for home. I had spent quite a bit of time in my tree, and the sun was melting into the horizon, turning the sky a dark shade of purple with mixtures of red and blue fading with the sun's descent. Any sort of animal could be tracking me. At that moment, behind a group of trees behind me came what sounded like a chuff. *Is that the same family of unicorns from this morning?* I walked over to them slowly.

"Where are your parents? Did they run off to get food?" The young unicorns seemed frightened, so I kneeled down and held my hand out to show I meant no harm. The creatures must have understood because the next moment, they were right in front of me, butting my hand as if they wanted me to pet them.

"Is everything all right?" I asked gently.

"*Chuff, neigh, neigh.*"

"I wish I could understand you, little ones. It will be completely dark soon. I better head home while I can still see the path." I turned to walk away, even though something didn't feel right. Still, I had to get home. Hopeful that the little creatures were fine, I continued walking along the path and unfortunately snagged my tunic on a branch, causing it to rip.

"Great, now I need to find some orange thread and a needle. Or a good seamstress."

The following morning came a very unsettling feeling. I couldn't stop thinking about the young unicorns being alone. It seemed to be such a small matter to worry about, but my mind wouldn't let them escape. They wouldn't survive on their own just yet, would they? They were still too young. There is no way the parents would leave their young ones to find food or water.

Should I investigate? No. Not alone. My tracking skills are about as high as a blade of grass. Wait, why am I even thinking of going back? Why would I care? The young unicorns are big enough to provide themselves with food and water...right?

I couldn't find the right words to justify not caring for the creatures. Truth was, I did care. I was too afraid to admit that something wasn't right. I walked over to my window as I ran through the thoughts in my head, the unnerving feeling I've had recently. As I approached the window seal, I was overtaken by the breathtaking beauty painted across the sky. I put aside the worry for a moment and headed to get a satisfying meal for breakfast. The sunrise was soft, smooth, and brightly colored blue, with a mix of red, yellow, and orange. Calm and jubilant. This made the mood a little easier as I walked to Mr. Malik's. Arriving at the market, there was a crowd of people outside, acting confused and mad.

"What's going on?" I pushed through the small crowd gently and tried to open the door. "It's locked. Where is Mr. Malik?" I peered through the window in search of any sign as to where he might be. No sign of him or where he is. Anywhere.

"Seems that he went off on one of his random vacations. Y'know, like he does every few months," Shalon said hopefully.

A stream of "yeah" echoed through the crowd. *Mr. Malik was on vacation just two months ago. Why would he be gone again in such a brief time? Do we, the village, eat here so much that he has to go to a new place to find relaxation every couple of months now? Seems strange, but I suppose it's possible.*

Midafternoon, a couple of days later, most people were busy with skill-set jobs or activities, bringing income to support themselves and their families if they had any. That skill set job for me...taking out the trash for various restaurants and merchants in the village. Someone had to do it, right? Walking briskly, pushing a wheelbarrow load of trash from Vandra's eatery, I noticed a figure standing next to a tree on the edge of the Forest. Almost as if it were wanting me to approach it. But standing what seemed to be over a hundred yards away, I couldn't make out what the figure was.

After a moment, which seemed to last an eternity, "Torren! Get moving! There's more that needs to be taken out!" Vandra yelled, startling me and causing me to turn over the wheelbarrow, spilling trash everywhere.

"Yes, ma'am!" I yelled back. The figure was gone. Was I seeing things? Was it my imagination? Something wasn't adding up. In just a couple of days, the strangest days of my life had occurred. The unicorns, the disappearance of Mr. Malik, which most would say is nothing out of the ordinary, the feeling of someone watching, and that figure across the way. Where did it go? I placed the trash in the village trash disposal, put the wheelbarrow back in its place, clocked out for the day, and went straight to Miri.

Miri had just clocked out when I arrived. Remember when I said Miri found her calling early on? Well, she can move objects and has a very keen eye for decorating and building. Lucky for her, the village is always looking for some type of architectural upgrade or home decoration.

"Mir! We need to talk," I said frantically, walking toward her. "I feel like I'm going insane! Sort of. I'm seeing things, I'm hearing things, there's no way that Mr. Mal..."

"Torren! Torren! That's enough!" Miri stopped me. "Mr. Malik is fi— Oh. Hang on." She looked at me intensely. "Is that... soup in your hair?" She reached up and pulled out some makian soup from my hair, which stuck out like a sore thumb in my red hair. "There. Anyway, I'm sure Mr. Malik is fine. And I'm sure you're just overthinking things like you always do. But entertain me, what do you mean exactly?"

"I just, I...Well, Miri. I'm not sure." Now, Miri handed me a cup of fresh mushroom coffee.

"Just relax, take a breath. When you feel up to it, we can talk about it. Obviously, you're too shaken to speak just yet," Miri said calmly.

"Thank you," I said, "I'm good." I paused for a moment. "So, for the past couple of days, I've felt there has been a pair of eyes watching, not necessarily me, but the whole village. And when I'm in the Forest, I hear footsteps and twigs breaking but see no one." I stalled, waiting for a response from Miri. She sat silently, almost confused. "Then, the day I came back from hunting, I spotted a family of unicorns, a mother and three calves. They were marvelous to see. Never, in my life, have I seen a family of unicorns by the river on the west, just on the outskirts of town."

"Why would a family of unicorns be that close to town?" Miri asked.

"Exactly. Why? And then the next day, I saw the same family, only the mother wasn't with them," I said.

"Well, that is pretty odd. Maybe she was going for food, or maybe the colts were old enough to be on their own," Miri said, sounding unsure of her response.

"And Mr. Malik would not go on vacation; he practically just returned from one not long ago. I hate to say it, but we need to look into all this."

Just there, we heard a voice call out to us, "Torren! Miri! Am I glad I found you." It was Cormac. Cormac Chalperus had been our friend for a few years now. He was one of the best steel workers you'd find. Trustworthy and strong, he knew how to work hard and always got the job done; although he wasn't the smartest elf, but the elf could make anything you asked with a good flame and some metal. He was a bit on the heavier side, but don't let that fool you; he was in better shape than me.

"Cormac! It's nice to see you!" Miri said, almost half shockingly.

"We were just talking about…uhh…hunting," I stumbled on words, searching for an excuse.

"Yeah, you are talking about hunting nothing. You were talking about Mr. Malik."

"How could you have guessed that, Cormac?" I asked, surprised at his perfect guess.

"Almost everyone in town is speaking about it. It's strange, isn't it?"

"At least I'm not the only one thinking it," I said. "Told you, Miri."

"Well, that settles it, we investigate!" Cormac exclaimed.

"No! We will not be investigating! We wait for the properly trained personnel to start a manhunt if it's warranted, which it's probably not," stated Miri.

A moment of silence passed, with the three of us staring blankly at one another.

"I vote that we take the night and sleep on it, meet at my place for breakfast, and discuss the matter then. Deal?" I suggested.

"Fine with me," Cormac said.

"All right, I guess that works," said Miri, slightly dissatisfied.

"Great. See you for breakfast. I'll cook something... delicious."

"No!" they both yelled quickly.

"Don't worry about the food. I'll bring something," Miri suggested.

Later in the evening, I couldn't eat. My nerves were too... bent out of shape, wrecked, to a point, at the thought of what we may find *if* we all agreed to adventure, to something that we knew absolutely nothing about. All I could do was pace around my cottage. Chores had been neglected the entire day. I was so exhausted, but the thought of sleep...well, I couldn't even think about a good night's rest. My mind wouldn't allow such a thing now. Still, I knew I had to at least put some form of good energy in my body, so I grabbed a fig and a handful of nuts and berries. I happened to look out the window and see the sunset. It seemed almost like a nightmare. The color of smooth red setting against a dark, grayish blue sky; not the usual pleasant, relaxing scene we were used to here in VaHaile. A storm rolling in, maybe? In a way, I guess it was sort of...beautiful.

When morning came, I felt certain, calm, and like I knew what needed to be done. I didn't sleep well at all, but I had this burst of energy out of nowhere. So, I decided to finish the chores I had left undone yesterday. I had just finished when I heard a knock. I had lost track of time picking up and scrubbing the floors, but I was thankful I had done so because that must be Miri and Cormac. Thank the High Elf. As I started opening the door, Cormac aggressively pushed through and let himself in. His manners were almost nonexistent, but he made up for it in brains and humor, I supposed. Miri, on the other hand, waited patiently to be let in.

"Come in," I say, enthusiastic.

"Someone's in a chipper mood this morning," Miri said, noticing the smile on my face.

"Yeah, what happened to Torren the worrier?" Cormac said playfully.

"Guys, I don't really. It's just like, like something awoke in me this morning. I can't explain it. But I know what we're supposed to do."

"And what might that be, Torren?" Miri asked.

"Go to Mr. And Mrs. Flantly. They're the oldest and wisest elves in the village. If there is something suspicious going on, they'll know what to do."

"But how would they know anything? They mostly stay at home now, cook, clean, tend to their garden and call it a day. Though I will say, they make the best coffee in the entire village, so I'm down," Miri said. Cormac agreed.

"Well, that was easier than expected," I said.

We ate our breakfast, which consisted of strawberry jam, bread that had a soft center but a very satisfying crunchy outer shell, some eggs scrambled to perfection, bacon, briskberries, and our favorite: coffee. We finished eating the delicious food, chatted for a while, and just before lunch, we headed out to the Flantlys' place. They lived close to the high elves' castle, in a section of the village named Eru Psyawla. Royal elves, their families, and their closest friends lived there. The Flantlys used to babysit for the High Elf, Ralcord, and gained so much respect from the arrangement that they, too, earned a spot in Eru Psyawla.

All of Zynthia is beautiful and unique. Lined with rich heritage and wonderful craftsmanship. You'll not find anywhere in the world where the woodwork is so elegant and smooth. So, imagine how beautiful a place where the High Elf resides is. The journey isn't far; it's just a day's travel, maybe a little further on foot. There are guards wandering the area, but they don't question most who walk through. Inside Eru Psy, short for its true name, Eru Psyawla, there were markets and merchants, but much bigger and fancier than that of Zynthia. It would come as no surprise that these items were a bit pricier. By now, it was just after lunch, planned perfectly to arrive in hopes of a well-cooked meal made by Mrs. Flantly, better known as Nance. *Knock. Knock. Knock.*

"I hope they don't mind us being here during lunch," I said quietly, as I knocked sternly but gently at the door so as not to seem rude but loud enough I thought they'd notice. The Flantlys were old, but I was not so certain how well they heard.

"Why, hello there. We've been expecting you," said Mr. Flantly.

"What do you mean, expecting us?"

So, remember when I mentioned elves having gifts? Well, there is another form of gift some elves possess. The ability to feel the future. No, it's not that they know exactly what will come to be, but they feel the energy that an event, item, or person will bring. Especially ones that have a big influence in a certain place in time. And once that person, item, or event is near, they get the feeling again, only stronger.

"You see, young elves, I know you've heard of the gifts and power all sorts of elves wield. I just happen to be an elf who can feel what will come," he said. "Though I am uncertain as to why you are here, I am certain that you are meant to be here."

"I think I understand, Mr. Flantly," I said.

"I think they're both crazy," Cormac whispered to Miri. Miri chuckled softly.

"*Shhh,*" Miri replied.

"Well..." Mrs. Flantly found her way into the conversation. "Don't just stand around. Take a seat; it sounds like you may be here a while," she said as she handed us all a fresh cup of mushroom coffee from a serving tray.

She then went back into the kitchen and came right back out with another tray of sandwiches. *They did know we would be here today. Huh. Imagine that.* There were enough sandwiches for everyone to have two if they desired. After eating lunch, which was delicious, we discussed our reasoning for being in their home.

"Well," Mr. Flantly paused. "I believe you follow what you feel. Follow your heart. I think you'll find, even if the path is frightening, the bond along the way and the fruit at the end are well worth it," Mr. Flantly said.

"So, we are supposed to look into what's happening around the village? Investigate?" I asked, almost trembling.

"I knew it! I told you; we will investigate!" Cormac said, almost jumping for joy over the excitement of looking for adventure.

"Calm down, Cormac. No one said that we are, though I feel it's what we should do." I looked over at Miri as I finished my sentence, looking for some sort of assurance.

Miri crossed her arms and nodded her head to say, "You're right, Torren."

Rushing back to the village, a strong, devastating feeling overcame me. It stopped me in my tracks.

"Hey, are you okay?" Miri asked. I couldn't walk any further. "We're halfway between VaHaile and Eru Psy, Torren. We can't stop here. It's almost nightfall."

"Just give me a moment, Mir," I cried as I scanned the forest. "There's something here, following us, I think."

"Yeah! Which is why she said we can't stop here! Something is going to have us for dinner!" Cormac exclaimed loudly.

"Well, if it didn't know we were here before, now it does! Thanks, Cormac!" Miri said angrily. Just then, past a thicket of bush and tree, was a figure, the same figure I saw when taking out the trash the other day. *Is that...?* No. It couldn't be. The creature lunged forward, leaping over the ticket of bushes and passing by the trees. It charged faster, and just before reaching the path in which we stood, it stopped. Miri, Cormac, and I stood frozen in fear and silence. The night had blacked most of the world around us, and just a glimpse of light from the stars and the moon shined to guide us. Yet it was light enough to see that this may be our first and last adventure, if that is what you'd call our walk to the Flantlys' home.

"Torren, what do we do? What is it?" Miri whispered, trembling.

"I...I...I think it's a...unicorn?" I stuttered, uncertain. The creature then stepped two steps closer, just enough to catch more light.

"A black unicorn!?" Never had we seen a black unicorn. *Ever.* Stories of such creatures had been told, but we had never thought them to be true. In some stories, they were harmless, but they wouldn't attack. But the worst stories told they were bloodthirsty beasts just waiting to impale their victims, tearing them limb from limb and devouring what was left. We did not wait to find out which side of the beast we were confronted with. We ran as fast as we could, following the path to the village. The sound the beast made while it followed sounded like a sick, dying unicorn who ate a cat and a screaming woman. It is a hard noise to describe because there is no sound like it. But I will never forget it. After running for what felt like twenty miles, though in reality, it was only a couple at most, we no longer heard the creature behind us, but regardless, we dared not stop running.

Finally, we made it home. Exhausted slightly, as even the weakest elf is very athletic, but scared beyond belief.

"What...*in the dragon fire*...was that?!" Miri shouted while catching her breath. The villagers were nestled in their homes, preparing for bed or some sort of indoor activity by this time of the evening. A few elves, on the other hand, had decided it would be a good time to play Shadow Hunter. A game where one person chases a handful of peers with a lantern, trying to make the light touch them. The first person tagged with the light is the next person to be "it." But that's not the hardest part of the game. The hardest part is trying to find the group of friends who are hiding from the light. Okay, so now was the perfect time to be playing, except that meant someone more than likely had heard us running and screaming through the woods.

"What's going on?" Kyna asked. Kyna, Keela, Lorcan, and Aevin were cousins. Lorcan, the oldest of the bunch, was exceptionally well with a bow. He, like most elves, was very fit and athletic, as you should be as a skilled archer and hunter. He had blonde hair down to the base of his neck and green eyes. Kyna and Keela were twins, twenty years of age, who, quite frankly, are two of the nicest women you'll ever meet. Both with yellowish-red hair, almost like a sunset, long and braided. Keela kept her braid to the left; Kyna's braid lay to the right. It was one way to tell the twins apart, that, and that Kyna had a small patch of freckles on her left cheek. They both were exceptionally good with a blade. You wanted sparring partners? You wanted these sisters on your side. Aevin, one of the tallest elves in the village, was very skilled in art. He could draw or paint anything. Wanted a sculpture made for a party? He was your elf. Anything involving creativity. He would make it, create it, and it would be outstanding. And he was the youngest of the four, only nineteen.

"There...it's nothing, only a bee," I suggested.

"Bees, at this time of night? Yeah, right. And I know you freak out and worry about everything under the sun, but not even you run like that over a bee," Keela stated.

"Bllaaahhh," a billy goat belted. We all jumped and laughed.

"Johnny, what are you doing out of your bin, you blasted troublemaker?" Kyna said as she walked towards Johnny to put him back in his bin. We know we saw a unicorn, a black unicorn. But why was it so...distraught, so ominous? And why did I feel such sorrow, such pain, when it came near?

"What do you think of having some bread with a hint of mixberry jam?" Cormac asked.

"Mmmm, I think it'll do. It's about all I have. Torren, you want some?"

"No thanks," I replied. "I'm not very hungry." I was still feeling down about the night before, not much of an appetite.

"Well, what's wrong with you?" Miri asked. "Don't tell me. You're still upset about last night's adventure with that unicorn?" Miri said sarcastically. She was right. It isn't like it had followed us home, ran us down, and decided to have us for a late-night snack.

"Okay, I guess you have a point. Cormac, make me some too, please."

Cormac made the bread with jam. We all ate and drank our mushroom coffee and honestly just relaxed a bit. We still had to do our duties of the day, but neither of us had the energy to do them yet. Suddenly, a very loud, strong *knock knock knock* came at the door.

"Well, who could that be?" Miri asked as she walked briskly to open the door. "What are you doing here? Come in, I guess. It is raining outside."

"Thank you." It was Kyna, Lorcan, Aevin, and Keela.

"How kind of you, Miri," Kyna said as she skated by Miri. Generally, elves are kind, gentle folk. Very respectful. But on occasion, they hold a grudge. You see, when Miri and Kyna were younger, Kyna was jealous of Miri because she had magic. It wasn't entirely her fault. Kyna's parents would always tell her how special she was. That she would, one day, have a gift that would bring much joy to the village. But when Miri possessed her power of telekinesis, Kyna just lost it. They were best friends, and Miri couldn't understand what made her turn against her. They squabbled here and there, nothing too harmful. But Kyna just always knew how to press Miri's buttons. Nonetheless, they could still get along if the need was pressing enough. It would, however, be far better if Kyna could just talk about why she resented Miri so much.

"We know you saw something last night," stated Aevin.

"A unicorn! A black unicorn!" Cormac shouted with much enthusiasm.

"*What?!*" exclaimed Kyna.

"Okay, we don't know if it was a unicorn, or if it was black," I said. "Regardless, it's not here now. There's no need to worry about it. Whatever it was."

"No, no, no. There is a need to worry. Don't you know?" Aevin said as he pulled out a pad of paper and a pencil. "A black unicorn is a cursed unicorn. Evil in every way that a white unicorn is beautiful. A horn that seeks blood, but not just any blood. The blood of an elf," he explained as he drew on his pad of paper.

"Those are only stories that adults tell children to scare them. To keep them from going near unicorns," Keela said.

"But is it just that, stories?" Kyna asked. "I mean, think about it. These stories have an awful lot in common with our history.

The writings about war with werewolves at the library. Do you remember?" Kyna continued. "That during the battle, certain humans could use magic, but only dark magic. They used their skill to turn unicorns against each other and, most of all, to hunt the elf it once called friend."

"That's right, Kyna. They thought they had the upper hand in battle once they learned magic," Cormac said. "But the Dragon Kingdom intervened. Said it was disgraceful that any race would use such a majestic creature to spill blood. Thus, we have a truce between elves and humans."

"Don't forget the wolves," Kyna said.

"Yeah, but didn't they just kill or eat anyone or anything on the battlefield?" Cormac asked.

"Well. No. They were hired by the humans to assassinate elves. Mostly high elves. They were exiled to Tenebrae for their erratic behavior and ruthless, barbaric actions during the war. The humans were given their own land to pursue and inhabit. Manthia"

We all stood quietly for a moment.

"So, who wants to hunt down a cursed unicorn?"

CHAPTER 2

Troubled Travels

After a few days, Mr. Malik still had not returned to the village. If he had, why would he not open his bakery or return home? His wife, Anwyn, had said he was supposed to be gone in just a couple of days. It was strange, she told us. We felt it, too.

"It wasn't like him to stay away any number of extra days. He'd miss me so much. Not to mention feeding the town folk his delicious breakfast," she said. And she was right. He cooked one heck of a meal.

Later in the afternoon, the seven of us decided to gather a few essential items, such as food and water to drink. Most importantly, other than Lorcan's bow and quiver of arrows and the twins' blades, we packed fresh coffee. Nothing beats a good cup of coffee. We agreed it'd be best to search for Mr. Malik first. A person is more important than a unicorn, cursed or otherwise. My mind, however, couldn't escape the feeling the creature gave me that night. Lonely, cold, and sad. A hunger for love and warmth. Desperate. Could it be the mother of the colts I had seen in the forest a few days ago? As we walked toward the forest, my heart raced. I started to sweat, and my legs felt weak. But I was thrilled and joyful to be on this journey. Not afraid, like some might think. But it was weird at the same time. The scene surrounding us was ecstatic. The wind was at our back. The sun was shining, but clouds hung, scattered along the blue sky. Like cotton flowers flowing in a blue river. Relaxing. Calm and, above all, hopeful. I felt that this was where *we* were meant to be.

As we entered the thicket of trees and bush, Cormac started singing.

"Well, the winds have come along, echoing our very call. The sky above holds the truth for us. How high we go, how far we stroll, our strength shall grow..."

"Cormac! Could you stop? The words aren't terrible, but your voice is deadly," Keela grumbled. We all laughed except Cormac.

"I just felt that a good journey amongst friends deserves a traveling song. What's wrong about that?" He said.

"Nothing except the sound of your voice, Cormac," I said. "Like Keela said, it's deathly. To be fair, none of us were gifted a singing voice."

Mrs. Malik had told us that Ren wanted to do some relaxation and sightseeing just out past the Druslan River, which is to the west of the village. The river begins on the Aztrean Mountain range, named after the dragon king, Aztrean, several hundred years ago. The river runs nearly strictly west until it hits Tenebrae. From there, it turns slightly east, heading south, emptying into Lake Jubilee. The second river, which travels along the eastern side, is named the Kymn River. Its headwater is believed to be the same as the Drulsan River. Nobody knows where it travels completely. Both these rivers are named after two of the bravest elves Zynthia had known. They were killed defending against the humans many years ago, but they played a big part, if not the biggest, in turning the war.

"But why would Ren travel beyond Druslan River? That leads to Tenebrae," Kyna mentioned.

"Well, it is beautiful…until you reach Tenebrae," Lorcan said. Tenebrae, a dark, ash-covered wasteland where its name comes from, with dying trees that have weak branches that hardly have any leaves. The sky is always gray, giving off a shade of purple and red as if it were tainted with blood and sin. A slight fog blankets the cold, wet ground, which reeks of sulfur and blood. No one dares step foot in Tenebrae alone. Some say the land is cursed, like the werewolf's heart. Dark and evil. Whether it be myth or fact, you'd be a fool to want to find out by yourself.

"But why, then, did the werewolves seem to get the worse end of the deal *if* they were hired *by* humans?" Keela asked.

"Good question. Good question, indeed," I responded.

The path to Tenebrae is a couple of days, at best, on foot. According to Anwyn, her husband was camping a half-day journey from Tenebrae, usually a safe distance from the cursed land. Werewolves don't stray too far from their village. If they do, it's said they would keel over on the spot or become gravely ill from the curse cast by…well, the stories never say who actually cast the spell. Dragons are magical, but it's never been mentioned they cast spells.

"We should reach Ren in a couple of days or so," I said. "*If* our calculations and information are correct."

"What will the High Elf say?"

"What do you mean, Kyna?" Lorcan asked.

"Well, the seven of us just left on an adventure, and we will be gone who knows how long. What if they send a search party for us because they believe we've gone missing, as well?"

"I mean, we did inform Mrs. Malik. And I told Mr. Frendon that I was taking a leave for a few days," I explained. "So, if we *do* go missing, the High One forbid, will no one be looking for us because they believe we are on holiday to relax?"

"Okay, it sounds bad when you say it like that, Keela, but I'm sure we will be fine," Miri added. We continued onward through the forest. The terrain was just like you'd expect a forest to be: some stones, twigs, dirt and trees, an occasional hill, and a small valley. The first day of travel was beautiful. Nothing too rough. The sun had been out most of the day. The breeze was calm and soothing. The creatures that inhabit this section of the wood didn't pester us. We didn't pester them either, so it was a mutual understanding, I suppose. Most people never travel beyond this point, so we weren't sure what to expect going forward. We came to an area with five decently sized stones, just big enough to sit. The trees were spaced a bit further apart, creating a perfect view of the sky above while creating enough cover to keep us mostly dry if it started to rain, and it looked like that was what was about to happen. We decided it would be a good stopping point and set up camp. It was getting dark, and we were all getting hungry, anyway.

"I've been here, once, with my parents as a child," Lorcan told us as the rain drizzled down lightly. "They were teaching me how to hunt. I got my first slorg right over there." He pointed to what seemed to be a bush just to the left of a hawthorn tree. "I was so excited, I ran to the slorg, barely noticing my surroundings, and tripped over a branch the size of my leg," he said while chuckling. "I didn't care, though. I had just had my first successful hunt," Lorcan came from a family of hunters. Skilled archers, he and his parents. Some said that Lorcan was the best archer that Zynthia had seen in hundreds of years, and I believed it. He was always precise. He could read the wind around him and almost curve the arrow in such a way it was like he was the arrow. Always hit the mark.

"I've never been to these parts of the forest," I added. "First time for everything."

"Except for you having a successful hunt or cooking a decent meal, Torren," Miri teased. The others laughed, and I gave her a slight smile.

"*Ooh*! She got you there, man," Cormac blurted loudly.

"Hey, why don't you wake the whole blasted forest while you're at it, Cormac," snarled Kyna, looking up to the sky. "It's getting late, we should sleep." We didn't realize it had gotten so late and that the rain had stopped.

I climbed up a tree, almost to the top, as the others were making their beds for the night. The clouds were leaving, and the twinkle of stars lined the dark sky that hung over us. It was amazing. I haven't star-watched in what felt like ages. As a child, my dad and I would sit out front of our house and make images out of the stars, almost like a connect-the-dots game. He would explain how the stars can lead us at night, like a road, if we were ever lost, and that the moon is like a giant lantern in the sky to light our way. My mind was reverting back to that time, and I began to daydream, when suddenly a whisper in my left ear shook me, almost out of the tree.

"Hey, you!" It was Miri. "I'm sorry, I didn't mean to scare you. Can I join you?"

Still dazed from her startling greeting and almost falling from a tree, I replied, "I don't think there is room for both, maybe right there." I pointed to a branch that was just to the side and a little below mine.

"Works for me," she said as she lightly plopped down on the branch. "It's pretty amazing, isn't it?" she said. Looking out into the dark wood.

"It is," I replied, looking at her. I quickly looked back to the sky. "It glistens so perfectly, not too bright, but still bright enough to get lost in the darkness that surrounds it. But not in a sad sort of way. In a peaceful, more calming way."

"Yeah, I think I know what you mean," she said with a slightly confused look on her face. Maybe it made sense? To me, it sounded right. I've never been great with words, but sometimes you just can't explain a feeling or mood with words. I thought to myself.

"Come on, dreamer, we need some shuteye for the trip tomorrow. A long way to go still," Miri said while climbing down the tree. I followed after her, made a bed of fallen leaves and some old blankets I'd brought, covered with my cloak, and fell fast asleep.

In the morning, I awoke to a young cadax, sort of mix between a dog and cat, a very friendly creature, with orange fur, a tiny white patch on the top of its head, and long zigzag stripe running down its back.

"Good morning to you, too, little friend," I said while yawning. "Wake up! Good morning, fellow travelers!" I shouted cheerfully, thinking that would wake my slumbering friends. Unsuccessfully, they continued to snooze. I then proceeded to walk around and shake them individually. To no avail, I decided to change my approach.

"*Ahhhhh!! Get them off! Get them off!*" I screamed, moving around frantically as if I had varhics all over me. Varhics are small insects, like spiders, but with two legs, a stinger on the front of their head, and sleek black fur covering their bodies. They are slightly venomous, but not enough to kill an elf, but it was one of the most painful stings one would ever feel. I continued, "Varhics, everywhere! *Help! Help!*" And with that, everyone jumped up, shaking vigorously and shouting all sorts of curses. I stopped and laughed as I watched them all dance around, all crazy-like. After a few seconds, they realized I had tricked them, and there were no varhics.

"Very funny, Torren. Very funny," Lorcan said as he threw his dark blue cloak in my direction.

"What are you thinking, Torren, scaring us like that? It's not funny," exclaimed Miri, obviously annoyed. "Since we are all up, who's hungry?"

"I could eat!" said Cormac, excitedly. With that, we all grabbed some snacks we had in our packs and made coffee with a travel pot and press that I had brought. Lucky for us, Keela had brought some eggs, safely wrapped in cloth, inside a wooden container to help protect them.

"You brought eggs?" Kyna sarcastically asked her sister.

"Best to be prepared. We got to eat, don't we? It isn't much, but it'll last a couple of days if we use them sparingly," replied

Keela. We ate our breakfast and cleaned up quickly. We still had a good way to go before reaching Mr. Malik's supposed campsite, so we all wanted to start walking sooner rather than later.

Treading up a small hill, not long after we started walking, we approached what looked to be an old campfire pit, some rustled leaves and branches, and two spots on the ground that looked as if that's where people had slept.

"Was Mr. Malik traveling alone?" Kyna asked. I scanned the area suspiciously and scratched my head.

"Maybe this isn't from Mr. Malik," I stated.

"Then who else could have been here? Another search party?"

"Who knows?" said Miri. "Maybe we'll find out soon enough."

"I suppose you're right. But we need to keep moving," Kyna stated. We hiked down the other side of the hill, surprised that it was a bit steeper. About halfway down, Keela tripped, lost her footing, and rolled head over heels toward the bottom of the hill.

"*Keela!*" yelled Kyna. Lorcan raced down the hill until he was parallel with Keela, who at this point was sliding, went down in sliding position, and grabbed Keela's left leg, now upside-down, halting her to a stop. Lorcan crawled beside Keela, looked over her for any broken bones, and then carefully picked her up and walked her down the rest of the hill.

"Keela. Are you okay?" Lorcan asked softly. Keela responded, but it sounded more like a low, rumbled, gibberish noise that a baby would make when trying to speak.

"It's okay, just breathe," Kyna instructed. "Just lay down and put this under your head." She lifted Keela's head gently and placed the folded cloak under it.

"What…what happened?" Keela spoke softly. "My head is killing me."

"You probably have a concussion. You need to just lay still for a bit and gather yourself," Lorcan said.

"I'm fine, really," Keela said, hopefully, trying to get up. "*Agghhh!*" she screamed. "On second thought, I'll stay right here." There was a brief silence. Everyone was distraught, not only because Keela had been hurt, but because she was in need of help we couldn't provide in the forest.

"Torren, we need to take her back to the village. She's broken her leg, and she has a concussion. There is no way that she can continue on this, possibly pointless, journey to Tenebrae."

"I know. I know," I told Kyna. "This is what we will do. Kyna and Lorcan, you both take Keela back to the village while the rest of us continue the journey to find Mr. Malik. We can meet at Miri's place in a few days."

"Okay, well, what if a few days pass, and you're still not back at the village?" Kyna asked.

"Well," I paused for a moment to think of a reasonable plan. "Then you come find us. Or else you explain to the High Elf, and he sends a search party. But we would probably face some sort of punishment for handling it ourselves. Either way, we still need to find Mr. Malik and get Keela to help."

"Done deal," Kyna responded. Lorcan, Kyna, and Aevin gathered leaves, things, a couple of big branches, and strings of bark from the wood, sounding us. Together, and surprisingly quick, they managed to weave a carrier just big enough to hold Keela. We helped load her onto the carrier, and then Kyna and Lorcan carried her off into the woods, heading for the village.

It was just after midday now. Miri, Aevin, Cormac, and I had not eaten since breakfast. We wanted to make up time for the accident earlier. I don't think any of us could think about food. We were all too worried about Kyna, Keela, and Lorcan, hoping they made it back to the village okay and that Keela received the care she needed. I hoped she was okay. It was a nasty fall down the hill. Elves are a tough breed, but even we break and bleed. I was surprised that it wasn't me who went barreling down the hill. After all, I am considered the clumsy one. After walking through the brush and thick trees until the sun was going down, we had made a good distance between us and home. We had come a long way, enough that we could rest and eat. We decided to call it a day and settle near a big oak tree, neighboring a small pond with dark green and brown colored water. I wouldn't suggest driving from it unless it were life or death. Cormac had sat against a large log next to the oak tree, taken out his pad of paper and feather quill, and started drawing. Miri had sat down beside me on the ground right in front of the pond, looking out to the forest ahead of us.

"You just going to sit there?"

"It's sort of gloomy, ominous, don't ya think?" Miri replied. "What do you think we will find out here?"

"I'm not completely sure, but I hope for a healthy Mr. Malik. Maybe I'll figure out who I am."

"You know who you are, Torren. You're a kindhearted elf who would do anything to help another and loves unconditionally. You always have others' needs before your own," Miri stated while placing her hand on my shoulder.

"You know what I mean, Miri. I'm the worrying, clumsy village elf that isn't good at anything."

"You're good at a lot of things, Torren. You're too hard on yourself. Just do the best you can do and move on. Besides, being extremely skilled is overrated."

"I mean, I don't see how it's overrated, Miri, but okay," I said. "But thank you for being a great friend, Miri." Miri pulled out some berries she had in her sack and held her out her hand, offering some to me. Not a bad way to end the day. Sitting there with Miri, sharing a snack, sitting by this pond. Were there any creatures living there? Hopefully not troublesome.

The following days were filled with scenes of trees that seemed to touch the sky with beautiful leaves, just changing color for the season, and meadows lined with various colors of pink, blue, and purple flowers that would put anyone in a good mood. It rained on occasion, filling the ground with mud. Lots and lots of mud. I, unfortunately, lost my right boot in a hole filled with water and muck almost as thick as tar. Thankfully, Aevin had thought to remember to bring a spare pair of boots. They were a tad too big, so walking was a little odd, but they did the job.

"We've been traveling for days, and still no sign of him," Aevin said. "What if we never find him, or worse, he's dead?"

"Wait. Everyone stop," I said quietly. There it was, the feeling of despair and loneliness. Longing for love. *The cursed unicorn. It must be close.* "Keep your wits about you."

"What do you mean? Torren, what's wrong?"

"It's nothing, Miri. We need to keep moving. We've got to be getting close to Tenebrae by now." And soon after we started walking, through bush and trees, just on the other side of a small meadow, hung Mr. Malik, suspended in the air by a net, as if someone had laid a trap and captured him.

"What in dragon's fire is he doing up there?" Aevin whispered. "Should we cut him down?"

"Yes, we should, but not yet. We don't know who set the trap or what danger there may be. We need to be smart about this," I said.

"It couldn't be the werewolves; they're not supposed to leave Tenebrae, and it's still a day's journey. Humans, you think?"

"I'm not sure, Miri," I replied. "Could be, but since the great war, they've not been known to come around Zynthia or Tenebrae."

"Whoever has him up there must come back to check on him. He's still obviously alive. I say we wait to see who it is that comes back, then make our move, or when they leave, we sneak over and cut him down," Aevin explained his idea. "Well, if we can get a little closer, I could use my power to untie the neat and gently let him down, hopefully. I've never used my ability on a person, just smaller objects."

"Well, he doesn't seem too high up, so the fall shouldn't be too painful," I said. We scanned the area and went around the meadow, behind the thickets of bush and trees in hopes no one would spot us. We were able to move within a few yards of Mr. Malik, and Miri attempted to free him. She raised her hand and lowered her chin to focus her eyes and mind on the knot, holding the neat closed. She grunted and moaned for a brief moment.

"I need to move a little closer," she said. We nodded in agreement and began moving when suddenly, we heard laughter and humming coming from the wood just behind Mr. Malik. It was a deep voice, but one we didn't recognize.

"*Hmmm. Ahmmm.* Ha-ha, my pal, Ren. How's it hanging?" a man said loudly as he appeared from the wood. It was difficult to see, but he appeared to have long black hair. His clothes seemed slightly tethered, dark colored; we couldn't tell the color due to the darkness surrounding him, and he wore a cloak laced with a silver trim that glistened in the moonlight. They chatted back and forth and seemed to be arguing, but we couldn't make out the words.

"Who is that?" Aevin whispered.

"*Shhh.* I'm trying to hear them."

"I can't hear anything, Torren."

"Well, Aevin, maybe we could if you stopped talking," I replied.

The man speaking to Mr. Malik occasionally spoke loud enough that I could make out a word or two, but not enough to make a sensible sentence. After a few minutes, finally a phrase we could understand came from the man.

"If you won't tell me where it is, there you're no use to me. You'll hang here until you starve to death." He walked back into the ominous forest behind him, disappearing into the darkness. We waited a few minutes to make sure it was safe to move and got close enough for Miri to untie the netting. As he untied the knot, Mr. Malik fell, but Miri was able to slow his momentum, lowering him safely to the ground. We ran to him as he lay confused, sprawled out on the dirt and grass.

"Mr. Malik, are you okay?" Miri asked.

"You shouldn't be here. He will kill you."

"We will worry about that later, for now, let's get back to the village," I insisted politely. We made it back across the meadow and about a hundred yards or so into the forest.

"Wait, wait! I need to stop a moment," Mr. Malik said.

"We need to keep moving, sir. What if he notices you're gone? He will hunt us down."

"We have time, trust me. He needs his rest as well."

"Here, you are probably hungry," Aevin said as he handed him some nuts and berries.

"Thank you," said Mr. Malik.

"Let's just get you home," I said. And as we moved along, we heard the faint sound roaring behind us, a sickly *neigh*.

"Move, now!" I shouted as I ran deeper into the forest, trying to escape what could only be the cursed unicorn. We didn't know for sure what it was, but we didn't want to find out. It sounded angry but ill. We didn't stop to sleep or eat; we just kept moving until, finally, the sun was starting to come up, and we no longer felt like we were being chased. We had been going all night. We were hungry, tired, and, most of all, frightened. We needed a hot meal and rest. A cup of warm coffee sounded wondrous right now, but we were too shaken to do anything but move forward. Finally, we came to a hawthorn tree, surrounded by a couple of stones and bushes, almost perfect for a moment to rest.

"We sleep here," I suggested. Even though the sun was rising, we nestled down beside the bushes and hawthorn trees and slept.

Meanwhile, Keela was receiving care from the village doctor, Dr. Smickel. She did indeed have a broken leg, a concussion, and a broken wrist. Kyna and Lorcan told Dr. Smickel they were playing a game of Shadow Hunter when Keela tripped over a branch and rolled down a slope, thus sustaining the injuries. Dr. Smickel may or may not have bought the story, but nonetheless, he didn't question them further. Lorcan brought a cup of coffee to Keela as she sat up in her bed, letting go a small *"Ahhh."*

"Thank you," she said.

"Easy now, it's hot."

"When do you suppose the others will return?" asked Kyna, sitting in the window just across from the room, sipping on her coffee.

"Hopefully, within a couple of days," replied Lorcan.

"Should we go back, maybe meet them halfway? If they're not in trouble," Keela asked.

"You, definitely not. Lorcan and I will wait another day or two and then discuss it. You need to rest." Keela laid back down and fell asleep. Kyna and Lorcan went out to the market to buy some berries, nuts, and dough to make mixberry cookies, some bread, and the ingredients to make makian soup. The soup would be better from Olive's, but they enjoyed the cooking and thought it would best to keep their minds off worst-case scenarios. Anwyn Malik knocked at the door just as the mixberry cookies had finished baking in the stone oven.

"Come in, Mrs. Malik. We have makian soup and some fresh cookies, if you'd like," Kyna greeted her at the door.

"Thank you," Anwyn replied. "But I don't want to bother you too long. I'm sorry that your searching for my husband got you hurt, Keela," she said as she placed her hand on Keela's hand.

"You don't need to apologize, Mrs. Malik."

"Please, call me Anwyn. I feel old when you say Mrs. Anwyn."

"That I can do," Keela replied. The three of them spoke to Anwyn most of the afternoon, explaining what we all saw on the journey until Keela's unfortunate event, of course. Kyna, Keela, and Lorcan didn't know that Mr. Malik was safely on his way home with Aevin, Miri, Cormac, and me.

"Between you and me," Mrs. Malik lowered her voice and motioned them closer to her, "I believe there was something suspicious going on with Ren. I questioned him about it, but he swore everything was all right. After the first couple of days passed and he still wasn't home, I knew something was wrong. I just couldn't place my finger on it."

"What you mean, Anwyn?"

"Kyna, this past year, he has always been going somewhere every couple of months. Usually, he'd return in a couple of days, but he would always seem sad or disappointed. It was highly unlike him to be upset about anything, especially returning home from a trip." Anwyn started to cry. "The thought that something has happened to him I...I just don't know what I'd do."

"I'm sure your husband and our friends are going to return any day now," Lorcan said, placing his hand over hers. "Kyna and I will search for them if they haven't returned in a couple of days."

"And, if you wouldn't mind explaining, a little more about this suspicious feeling you have?"

"Well, I mean, we all know he takes holidays every so often throughout the year, and usually he comes back with flowers for me or some type of craft souvenir that he made by hand on his journey. But this year, he'd return empty-handed, and he always acted as if he had done something wrong or...just not quite how Ren would normally behave. I can't quite explain it, but deep down, I believe something is wrong."

"I'm sure he's probably just tired from the travel," Kyna said.

"You may be right, Kyna. But either way, we can look into it more once they return," Lorcan added. "I better be on my way. I told Vandra I'd stop in and help clean up."

After she left, Kyna and Lorcan left a note by Keela's bedside that read, "See you in the morning. We will bring breakfast." Yum!

Somewhere in the forest, the rest of us hiked through, trying to reach the village. Mr. Malik seemed to be doing better after sleeping on the ground instead of a net and possibly eating better food than what he'd been fed prior to his rescue. This had been the most adventure that any of us had witnessed since ever. It was exhilarating but also very frightening. We were a day, give or take, from the village. The overwhelming feeling of sorrow still pitted my stomach. It'd been there since the night we freed Mr. Malik. There were no other signs of the unicorn, though; it had to be close. Aevin and Cormac had done their best to hunt two slorg, barely enough to feed all four of us. But it was better than the nuts and berries we had been eating the last couple of days. As we were eating our cooked slorg, we heard an echo of neighs, followed by roars screeching behind. We could hear the whimpering of the frightened unicorns get louder and louder as they quickly galloped towards us, one... two. Two unicorns, young and with barely any meat on them. They were the same young filly and colt I had seen that day by the river on my way home from the forest. I could tell because of the distinct golden line swirling down their horn.

You really are alone. I won't let you die, I thought as I stood up and walked briskly in their direction.

"Torren, what are you doing?!" yelled Miri.

"Follow me, guys; we have to save them!"

"You're mad! No way! Just let the vehuma have its lunch. Hopefully it leaves us alone!" Aevin said.

"Why risk your life for a wild unicorn, baby or grown?" asked Mr. Malik.

"I can't explain it; we just have to help them."

Miri stayed back with Mr. Malik while Aevin and Cormac followed me to a spot just behind a thicket of tall bush, a few yards from where the vehuma was antagonizing the two young unicorns, one of which was wounded on its left side, just above its front leg. The vehuma was also battered a bit, but a vehuma is relentless and will fight until either it succeeds in devouring its prey or its own death. Cormac and Aevin readied their small blades, which they kept in a sheath around their waist. Neither one was a master swordsman or exceptionally good with a blade, but they knew some techniques to survive. Against foes with two legs and normal teeth, that is. This, however, was a beast, about four feet in height and six feet in length, give or take. They had razor-sharp claws, as long as the palm of my hand, four of them on each paw, and hanging nails towards the back pad of their paw, slightly larger, sort of like a thumb. They had long tails that were just as strong as their legs, great for trapping their prey and squeezing the life from them.

"I'm glad you both have something useful. I'll be playing fetch with this stick." Just then, I noticed a dead tree lying beside me. I took the bark and the cambium layer between the bark and center and quickly wrapped them together, creating a rope, sort of.

"It'll do," I said as I pulled both ends simultaneously, testing the strength of my creation. "You ready?" I asked them nervously. They both nodded.

I took a stone and gestured for them to grab one near them; we counted to three, and we threw our stones at the beast to get its attention. It turned in our direction, sniffing, trying to catch our scent. It then lowered its head, let out a low, snarly growl, and headed toward us. We jumped out from the bush and quickly stood ready to be pounced on by the vehuma. But it stood still, staring at eyes, as if it was trying to decide which one to eat first, me, Cormac, or Aevin. The unicorns turned and ran full speed in the opposite direction. The vehuma turned its head, watching its prey escape, and quickly turned its head back to us.

"Man, I think it's angry," Cormac said. All of a sudden, it charged after us, leaping in the air right toward Cormac, who stood in the middle. I lunged at Cormac, tackling him into Aevin, knocking us, rolling down a small embankment, and evading the beast's claws.

"That was close," I said, terrified.

"Yeah, too close. What are we thinking?" Aevin replied.

"Here it comes!" Cormac threw his blade as the beast pounced in our direction, hitting it between the rib on its left side. Blood poured out, but the vehuma was still charging weakly now. We stood around the vehuma, circling and hoping to cause some confusion. It had its back to looking at me, looking right at me. It quickly turned its body, swinging its giant paw at Cormac, slicing his chest. Me and Aevin reacted quickly, without thinking, and jumped on the beast's back, hoping it wouldn't have a chance to finish Cormac off. Aevin, wrapping his legs around the beast, thrust his blade repeatedly. I had my rope around its neck, squeezing as tight as I could. The beast was going berserk, kicking back and forth, kicking front to back, trying with all its might to throw us off. Finally, it rolled onto its back, hoping to crush us. It was weak and close to dead. This was its only hope now. Frantically, Cormac leaped up, rushing to us with his small blade in one hand, the other hand on his chest where the beast slashed, and thrust the dagger into the vehuma's head, killing it instantly. Cormac quickly stepped to the side of the beast and aided in getting Aevin and myself out from underneath.

"Well, that was excitingly terrifying," I said jokingly. We sat right next to the carcass in silence for a moment as Mr. Malik and Miri headed to us.

"Cormac, are you okay?" Miri asked as she approached with haste.

"Cormac is hurt, but I don't know how bad," I replied.

"He barely got me, I believe," he said, uncovering the wound. It didn't look deep or like it had hit anything vital.

"It's not bad, but you'll still need to see Dr. Smickel once we get back."

CHAPTER 3

Welcome Home, in a Court Room

It was mid-morning the next day when we made it back to the village. A few villagers stared at us as we appeared from the dense wood. The look of awe and shock upon their face as they stood frozen at the scene which they were witnessing. A couple of villagers, Alistair and Croman, ran towards us and offered aid.

"A warm meal and a bath would be wonderful," Miri stated.

"I second that," Cormac grunted, feeling weak and sore from fighting the vehuma.

"He needs Dr. Smickel," I advised them. "It would do us good to see him too."

Anwyn came running, full speed towards us as she spotted her husband, cried out loud, "Ren! I can't believe my eyes!" and excitedly wrapped her arms around him, crying tears of joy. "Are you all right?"

"I'm fine, dear."

She looked in his eye, smiled, and said, "Welcome home."

"Torren Luxmin! What do you think you are doing?!" It was Vandra and Mr. Frendon, obviously distressed by my absence for the last few days. "Obviously, sightseeing wasn't the only thing you were doing!"

"Clearly."

"Guys, it's all right. We found Mr. Malik, and everyone is, well, mostly in one piece."

"Mr. Luxmin! Ms. Masel! With me!" Kulmond, father of Kyna and Keela, called out to us as they wheeled Cormac off to Dr. Smickel with the closest thing they could find, a wheelbarrow. Miri and I walked to Kulmond, not knowing what he was about to say or do or if he knew we were the reason Keela was hurt. Or worse, if he were going to tell us Keela had died from her wounds.

"Yes, sir?"

"What are you two, or however many went with you, thinking? Going off into the woods, toward Tenebrae!" Kulmond asked with extreme frustration. He had a right to be frustrated. Everyone did, honestly. Except for Mrs. Malik. She was grateful and joyous.

"Sir, we were doing what we thought was right."

"The right thing to do would have been to tell the High Elf your suspicions and let the Rangers handle the rest."

"But it would have taken days for the High Elf and the Council to vote on whether or not to search for Mr. Malik and then plan out the search. So, we just left. You know how they work."

"Because of you, my daughter lay in bed, wounded from joining on your little adventure."

"She is a grown elf. She can make her own choices, Kulmond. We didn't make her go."

"We will see what the High Elf and Council have to say. You simply can't skip the policy." With that, Fulmond stormed off, heading back to his shop.

"He's not completely wrong, y'know," I told Miri.

"And neither are you. It would have taken longer for the Council to put a search party together. Mr. Malik would've been dead. We did the right thing, Torren," Miri reassured me. "Can you believe he actually used your full name, though, Mr. Luxmin?" Miri chuckled. "Come on, let's go see the others."

Kyna, Keela, and Lorcan were outside the twin's house, watering the plants as we walked toward them quietly, hoping to surprise them.

"Hey guys!" Miri greeted them as we approached from behind Keela, who stood with support from a crutch. "How are you feeling?"

"Oh, my goodness!" Keela shouted, almost falling forward in shock. "You made it back! It's good to see you!" Miri and Keela hugged gently, knowing Keela would be sensitive to touch.

"I'm fine, Mir. Just a little broken and a headache."

"Where's Cormac?" Lorcan asked nervously.

"You guys missed out. We will explain on the way to Dr. Smickel. Cormac will be there, but don't worry; he should be fine." Miri and I proceeded to explain the events that occurred in their absence as we walked to go visit Cormac at Dr. Smickel.

"You saved baby unicorns from a vehuma?! Man, I wish I could've seen it! Those beasts are vicious but beautiful!"

"You're crazy, Kyna. Just like a vehuma. It was the scariest experience of my entire life," I said.

"So, who was the man that was speaking to Mr. Malik while he was captured?" asked Lorcan. "We couldn't tell. It was too dark. And his voice didn't sound familiar," I replied, and I started to knock on Dr. Smickel's door.

"Come on in, travelers," Ms. Smickel said, peering through the open window a few feet from the door. "It's unlocked." We did as we were instructed, let ourselves in, and walked to the center of the room, passing Ms. Smickel.

"Cormac is in the back with Dr. Smickel. He told us to be expecting you."

"Thank you," we replied as we walked to see our friend.

"There he is, the mighty vehuma killer!" Miri said, excited to see Cormac not dead.

"How bad is it?"

"It missed anything vital, Torren, and isn't very deep, so, overall, he's doing just fine," Dr. Smickel said. "I am worried, however, about the adventure you and your friends were tangled up in. I've been around a very long time, much like many others here in the village, including Mr. and Mrs. Malik. I'd be willing to bet that your adventure is just getting started."

"Why do you say that, sir?" Kyna asked.

"I believe what my husband is implying is that you should have told the High Elf and not investigated on your own. If you had, your friends may not be in the conditions they are in. And I say that respectfully."

"With all due respect, Mr. and Mrs. Smickel, they saved my life," Mr. Malik said, angered by the Smickels' comments.

"We don't mean to cause a ruckus, Ren. And I think you would think the same as we do, had it not been you in that net. The reasonable solution would be to let the Rangers handle the situation. But what will happen now that the man who captured you knows you have been rescued?"

We all stood in silence at the question. We haven't had time to fully grasp the events, or what will follow once we were home.

"That is something we now have to wait and see. But for now, let's just celebrate our victories."

The next morning, I was heading home from Mr. Malik's bakery, which he, to many people's surprise, opened, excited to greet and feed his customers, when I spotted two Rangers standing outside my home, knocking at my door.

"Excuse me, can I help you?" I nervously asked as I walked up to them.

"Are you Mr. Luxmin? Torren Luxmin?" one of them asked.

"That's me, sir," I stuttered. "Yes, sir."

"You're needed by the High Elf, along with your friends. He would like to speak to you about your recent adventures near Tenebrae."

"Yes, sir. Is everything all right, though? Are we in trouble?"

"That is to be determined, Mr. Luxmin." With that, we hurriedly went about the village, gathering the others. Kyna was not so easily persuaded. She argued with one of the Rangers, Nimion, until he had obviously had enough. He swiftly, but not violently, apprehended Kyna in one motion, putting her hands tied behind her back while she was mid-sentence.

"I'll have you thrown in," was all she blurted out. It was the fastest I'd ever seen an elf move. *Must be why he is a Ranger*, I thought in amazement. They walked us to the edge of the village where they had parked their wagon, pulled by domesticated unicorns. The wagon was white with shimmers of green trim laced with gold. The inside was padded with green walls, which had sketches of golden trees and vines on them. The seats were white with green and gold buttons throughout and wrapped around in a "C" shape. It would definitely fit us and one Ranger. It was a masterpiece.

"My father actually designed this particular model," Aevin pointed out gladly. This was a Royal transport carriage, not one made for prisoners. Those are black and gold, filled on the inside with bars made of stone and wood. Prisoner wagons weren't used often, at least not in our village. The driver commanded the unicorns to walk shortly after we were seated.

"Your father has good taste, Aevin," I said. The trip to Eru Psyawla was filled with tension, mostly from Kyna, who was obviously frustrated with being bound. She had done it to herself.

"So, Ranger…?" Miri asked, wanting to know his name.

"Vixwill. Ranger Vixwil," he stated. "But you can call me Dax."

"Well, Dax, we obviously don't seem to be in any real trouble, other than Kyna, of course, so why send for us to Eru Psy?" Miri asked.

"Ms. Masel, we were only told to bring you to the High Elf in the Royal Carriage." Miri sat back, disappointed in his reply. Thankfully, the scene on the way to Eru Psy was pleasing. The wind flowing through the window gave a nice cool breeze, lowering the temperature inside the carriage. It'd been miserable if the entire shell were enclosed, keeping the body heat in, and the sun beat down on the outer layer, creating a natural oven. We would be toast. The air was filled with the relaxing aroma of the forest and meadows of flowers we passed. Almost made me forget that we could be arrested once we arrived in Eru Psyawla.

"A beautiful day, isn't it?" I muttered to myself.

"What, Torren?"

"Nothing, Mir. I was just off to myself, talking and whatnot."

"*Oookayy*," Miri replied.

"I said it's a beautiful day."

"We're likely going to be arrested for being vigilantes, and you're saying you think it's a beautiful day?"

"You can't focus on the negatives, Kyna. You'll drown in darkness if you do."

"*Oh*, someone's getting deep, aren't we, Torren?" Lorcan commented playfully.

"No, seriously. Just look out the window. Regardless of what happens when we get there, it's still a good day. We brought Ren home safely, and everyone is alive."

"I guess you're right," Lorcan said.

We arrived in Eru Psyawla, at the High Elf Castle, in the early evening. It was awe-inspiring. We have been to Eru Psyawla before, but never this close to the castle. The Ranger who was driving the carriage got down from his seat, walked over, and let us out. We stood for a moment in amazement, asking what we were looking at. The history and the power that lay within the walls, the ground on which we stood. The outer walls were perfectly carved and placed pearly white stones, outlined in a beautiful green and gold banner, stretching along the top and bottom of the castle. The top seemed to almost touch the clouds, perfect for seeing out into the surrounding forest. We entered the castle through a huge green archway that shined with speckles of gold. I couldn't make out the material it was made from, but it was magnificent, nonetheless. The halls and ceiling were crafted of a mixture between white and green, with shades of blue swirling through, like a wave of water. We reached the Royal Courtroom and walked until we were about center in the room when one of the Rangers escorting us shouted, "Halt." We came to a stop and froze. Fear now sunk into the pit of my stomach, not knowing whether we would be prisoners here in Eru Psy for who knows how long or praised for our brave efforts of saving Mr. Malik. The High Elf and his Council stood up.

"Welcome to Eru Psyawla," the High Elf's wife, Valmera, said softly. She wore a lovely, white, long-sleeved dress with pink and green thread that intertwined upward from the skirt of the dress to the shoulders. "You all should be proud of yourselves. Because of your actions, an elf lives another day. And for that, the Kingdom of Zynthia is grateful."

The High Elf, Ralcord, who wore a white shirt underneath a green silk cloak trimmed in gold, of course, and had a white stripe running down the front, looked at his wife.

"But," he looked back at us, "you were terribly foolish. The Elven Rangers and the Council were created for such matters as a search and rescue. You nearly got yourselves killed," he pointed out angrily.

"Sir, if I may," I started to say when Valmera interrupted.

"You will have your turn, Torren. The rules are in place for a reason. For your safety, as well as that of Zynthia. Investigating, as you did on your own, was extremely dangerous, and not only for you seven." She pointed at each one of us and continued, "But for all of us."

"My queen is right. As she often is," Ralcord said. "Now, your side of the story."

"Sir, thank you. The plan was mine. I forced them."

"Torren, you idiot. Don't listen to him, High Elf. He doesn't know what he is talking about. We all agreed to go," shouted Miri, angry at my false confession.

"I did plan the journey, Miri."

"But we *all* agreed with it. You didn't force us," Kyna said.

"Is anyone going to tell the High Elf your side of the story, or are you going to fight each other and be arrested for assault on Royal grounds?" said Krilla, a member of the High Council. All the Council members wore either white or gold cloaks that had a green trim, and a green undershirt.

"Our apologies," I said, disheartened.

We proceeded to portray the strange feelings I was getting around the village, the unicorns, and what led to us looking for Mr. Malik. They listened intently, which honestly, felt good. It was great to know they were actually interested in what we had to say.

"For starters, when you, Torren, felt someone was watching the village, you should have immediately come to the Council. Secondly, there are no such creatures as cursed unicorns. Those stories are told to children for fun, and maybe to scare them. No one cursed anything or anyone except the land of Tenebrae, and rightfully so," explained the High Elf. "And even though you neglected to inform us of a possible threat to the kingdom, you were very brave. But that does not mean you escape punishment. You each will be confined to your village for one month. Not to even touch the edge of the forest."

"You mean I can't hunt?" Kyna exclaimed. "How will I eat? I don't make enough coin alone to feed myself and my sister, Keela, and she's not capable of work for the time being."

"The punishment is set. Do. Not. Leave. Your village," Krilla commanded.

"Easy, Krilla, they get the point."

"She really is a stickler for the rules." That was all. It seemed almost like a slap on the hand. I guess we should be grateful. The court had ended, and we were escorted back to the carriage.

"Well, it could be worse," Aevin stated while shrugging his shoulders.

"Shut up, Aevin," Kyna muttered, her hands still bound behind her back. She was still disgruntled, and I couldn't blame her. After all, she did make a good point for her side.

We returned to the village at nightfall. People outside stared at us as we exited the carriage. You could vaguely hear them whisper to one another, "What happened?" "What kind of trouble did they get into?" And "I'd hate to be related to them right about now." But it was fine. We knew that we did the right thing, helping Ren. I couldn't stop thinking about comments the High Elf made about the cursed unicorns and the things we were taught as children. I could swear those were mentioned in history books. In fact, I *knew* they were. I remember being in study, with Ms. Crosman explaining in horrific detail and crying her eyes out because her father had died during the war. She was just a little elf when her father was taken from her. Needless to say, she didn't teach history long and soon moved on to cooking. I had to go speak to her. But would she be willing? I knew I had to try, regardless. She's the only person who showed as much enthusiasm as heartache over the subject. She was passionate and, above all, seemed extremely educated in the matter.

I knocked at Miri's door early the next morning for several minutes. Finally, *"What do you want?! Let me sleep! The sun isn't even up yet!"* Miri shouted, obviously still in bed.

"Wake up, Mir! We need to talk!"

"Sleep! That's what we need!"

"But it's important, I swear!"

"Be quiet, you two! It's too early to be hollering at each other!"

"But you just started hollering back at them, and now I'm hollering at you! It's just a vicious cycle, so how about we all shut it!" Miri's neighbors joined the shouting.

There was a brief silence, and then, "This had better be good, Torren," Miri said while opening the door to let me in. "I was sleeping and having the loveliest dream," she expressed in anger.

"So, I was thinking," I started to explain as I walked to her kitchen to start making coffee, "You remember Ms. Crosman, who taught us history?"

"Yes, I think so."

"Well, you remember yesterday when the High Elf said the cursed unicorns and stories she taught, as well as the ones our parents taught us, were just... stories?"

"I was there, wasn't I? And he is probably right. You saw the one black unicorn, so you think. But just once. Not since then, and no one here in the village, other than Ms. Crosman, has mentioned a cursed unicorn seriously before. Just in stories," Miri said. She crossed the room hastily and acted as if she was upset. She muttered under her breath as she walked over to get a cup of coffee, but I couldn't make out what she said.

She sipped her cup of coffee and said, "That's more like it." And smiled. "We are quite the same, aren't we?" She asked with a smile.

"I mean, we're both elves. But what do you mean?" I was confused by her statement.

She chuckled. "Coffee, you goof. It's the first thing on our minds when we get up in the morning. Really, all day long."

"Yeah. That's true, but almost every elf loves coffee."

"Well, they don't drink it all day like we do. Besides, they're not 'Miri and Torren.'" She winked, took a sip of coffee, and cleared her throat. "Anyways, go on."

"We need to talk to her."

"We've only been confined for one day, Torren, and you want to go question the High Elf on what he said about our history, and not to his face, either? Are you looking for trouble? What if someone hears about it? Like one of the half dozen guards watching us?"

"No, Miri, I'm not. I just feel like maybe they are trying to hide something; maybe it's just to keep us safe, but we won't know unless we look into it. And it starts with Ms. Crosman," I said.

We stayed at Miri's place until around lunch, just sitting and playing a game of Stones and Sticks. A game with eight thick stones, bent and made in such a way that they bounce when hit properly, and two light round marble stones that had a slight bounce to them as well. The sticks are laid on the ground, standing in an arch form, and each player takes their stone and tries to hit the sticks up in the air and try to catch them. The first person to catch four sticks wins.

Miri won every time. Out of four games. I wasn't mad, though; I've never really been good at the game. I was just glad to have a time when I didn't think about the events from the last few days.

"That was my fourth win, Torren. Are you even trying to play?"

"Yeah, yeah. You know I'm not very good at Stones and Sticks. It is fun, though."

"If we're going to see Ms. Crosman, we ought to get going," Miri suggested. On our way to see Ms. Crosman, two of the guards from the Elven Rangers were whispering to one another, acting a little strangely. I would've just ignored it, but one guard spotted me and Miri, and suddenly slapped the other guard on the arm, pointed in our direction and then the two separated. Wonder what that was all about? Miri didn't even notice. Should I bring it up to her? Or am I being ridiculous? It was then, off to my right, I just barely caught a glimpse of two unicorns on the edge of the forest. They were looking right at me. I stopped walking and pulled Miri's arm, signaling for her to stop.

"What, Torren?" I pointed at the unicorns, and as Miri looked, they ran off into the trees. "What was that about?"

"I'm not sure. But I felt like they are trying to tell me something."

"Enjoying yourselves?" one of the guards who walked up asked.

"We're just out for a walk. Might go visit a friend," I replied.

"Just don't forget, No. Leaving. Town," the guard said sternly. Miri and I nodded our heads, acknowledged his words, and began walking again.

"You know you can't speak with animals, don't you? Though, you do seem to have some sort of connection with those unicorns."

"Well, we did save them. Look." I pointed to Ms. Crosman's house off in the distance. "Almost there." You could tell it was her house because of the antique trinkets on the lawn, perfectly aligned in chronological order. If there's one thing Ms. Crosman enjoyed more than baking, it was antique collecting.

Ms. Crosman was heading outside as we approached. "Hello, Ms. Crossman?" I greeted her as she was closing the door behind her.

"That's my name. Who might you be? Wait. Torren? Miri? Didn't I have you in class a few years back?"

"Yes, ma'am. History," replied Miri. "Is this a good time?"

"Well, I was just going to go pick some fresh briskberries. I plan to make a couple of pies later on. Is there something you need?"

"We just had a couple of questions, if that's okay."

"I suppose the berries can wait, come on in." We walked inside Ms. Crosman's house and instantly caught the scent of fresh homemade bread, biscuits, cookies, and other baked goods that she had prepared earlier in the day. It was pleasing and made me hungry, but I wouldn't ask for anything. Only if she offered. Which she did. We sat for a while and listened as she went down a rabbit hole explaining why she chose baking pastries and cakes over traditional cooking.

"I'm terribly sorry, I ramble a lot, and it just seems to keep going and going. Probably why people interrupt me more often than not. What were your questions?"

"You remember the lessons on the War for the Kingdom that you would get so...excited about?" I asked cautiously.

"Well, yes, what about them?"

"As you probably know, we were confined by the High Elf and the Council for not reporting the disappearance of Mr. Malik and some other events, yes?"

"I did hear that, and I am terribly sorry. You all deserve a medal or something. You were very brave. But what about these other events?"

"Well, I have been sensing someone close to the village, watching. Hearing footsteps in the woods but seeing no one. But the main reason we are here is because we, mostly me, have seen a black, possibly cursed, unicorn. In fact, one chased us through the forest," I replied.

"Or at least we are almost certain that's what it was," Miri added.

"*Oh*, my. It seems I should've kept teaching all along. But what does this have to do with, exactly?"

"During our meeting with the High Elf, he said the stories that we were told about unicorns being cursed and dark magic were all...children's stories. And I didn't think that's true. It can't be. Like I said, we are certain we encountered one. And I couldn't think of anyone else to talk to about it," I said.

"I don't know, you two. I can't go against the High Elf and the Council. But, and I swear, do not tell anyone that I am telling you this, *ever!*" she exclaimed. "But I know for a fact that dark magic and curses are real. The part I never told during my teachings was that as a little girl, I snuck out to go see my father during battle. I wanted to protect him somehow. I knew it was foolish, but we had this incredible bond, and I loved him so much."

Ms. Crosman began to cry. "So, I followed him, and everything was going well for a while. You should've seen him on his unicorn, with his sword. He was excellent. And suddenly, a man came out of the forest near my father. I'll never forget; he wore a dark cloak embellished with red, and his eyes were a mix of dark purple and red, kind of pretty, actually. He said something, but I couldn't understand it, and the unicorn threw my father off just across from me; then, it laid down and began to grunt and moan like I had never heard before. Before we knew it, its hair had turned black, and it stood up, angry, evil. It saw me first and charged right at me, but my father he...He jumped in front of me and was impaled by the unicorn. He was able to mutter run, Beatrice. So, I ran. So yes, for a fact, I know curses are real. But why would he lie to you?" Ms. Crosman said as she wiped tears from her cheek.

"Ms. Crosman, I am terribly sorry for what you witnessed all those years ago," I said. "I'm sorry that we made you relive that day, but I am grateful that you shared it. But now, what do we do?"

"You said that the unicorn didn't harm you, correct? It chased you, but what I know of a cursed one is that they are faster than a regular unicorn. I'm not saying that I doubt what you've told me or what you've been through," said Ms. Crosman. "But it is strange that you were not harmed. You and your friends are confined to the village, so I don't see what can be done for the time being. Just lay low and wait for this to pass, then come speak to me again, and we will figure something out."

It had been a few days after we had spoken to Ms. Crosman, and we felt hopeless. We had visited the others but weren't too comfortable with everything, being together for too long out of fear that the guards might suspect something. Cormac and Keela were healing well, but still, we didn't want them pushing their limits just yet. We had to plan carefully what to do next. What books or scribes could tell us what really happened on the battlefield all those years ago? Have they all been buried or burned? Surely not. They'd keep them somewhere safe, so if it were to happen again, they'd know what to do. They would have to be kept in Eru Psyawla. With these questions swirling in my head, I knew we couldn't wait any longer. We had to move. We had to act. I walked to Miri's house later in the day, but she wasn't there, so I walked to Kyna and Keela's place.

I knocked on the door, and Kyna shouted, "Just a second!" A few seconds later, she opened the door, "I knew it was you. Come in." She still seemed bitter over the confinement, but at least she let me in.

"How are you guys?" I asked.

"*Oh*, we're just lovely, Torren. Stuck in the village, no hunting or fishing. You know, usual confinement stuff."

Yeah, she is still upset.

"I'm sorry, Torren. I don't mean to be rude. I just love being out in the woods, trekking and hunting. Shooting a target that doesn't move gets rather boring."

"I understand, Kyna," I said. "It's okay."

"And how have you been?" Keela asked me as she handed me a cup of coffee.

"I'm...fine," I replied. "But...Miri and I, and do not tell anyone about this conversation, we talked to Ms. Crosman about the statements the High Elf made about the curses and battle for the kingdom."

"You did what?" Kyna exclaimed angrily. "You must love getting in trouble nowadays, Torren. What, confinement isn't good enough, so you're trying to get put in prison? Or worse?"

"No, Kyna. Just hear me out. If there's anyone in the village who knows more about this stuff, it's her. I don't like questioning the Council, but we know we saw a cursed unicorn. We had to talk to someone about it," I explained. "And she confirmed that cursed unicorns, black magic in general, is real."

"So, you tell us that you would believe an old history professor over the High Elf?"

"Normally, no. But this is her area of expertise. I believe her."

"No, Torren. You don't know that. She's crazy, mental. She'd lose her mind and start crying in the middle of class. That's why she didn't last very long," Keela said.

"That's just it. We all thought she was just loopy, but she had the right to be upset. She witnessed her father being impaled by a cursed unicorn. That's why she always got so emotional. Wouldn't you be overturned every time you had to relive an experience so...horrific?"

There was an awkward silence for a moment. The mood had been shot, filled with a looming sense of sorrow. We couldn't imagine seeing such an event. Seeing a loved one die right in front of us by one of the most majestic, magical creatures ever created.

"Who would do such a thing? Turning to dark magic. Killing a father right in front of his child?" Lorcan asked.

"Humans?" Cormac replied, shrugging his shoulders.

"The stories always said it was a human, but Ms. Crosman said the person she saw as a child wore a hood. She couldn't see his face clearly," I replied.

"So, how do go about investigating, or whatever you want to call it, this history mystery? Ha! See what I did there?" Kyna elbowed Lorcan after her clever rhyme.

"We can't march into the castle and just rummage through like we own the place. Besides, we're confined here. We can't leave," Miri said.

"What if we don't have to leave? There's bound to be a place where they would keep books or documents—something to account for the events from the wartime. A way to go back and learn from mistakes and successes in case a similar situation occurred. They would want to be prepared," I explained dramatically.

CHAPTER 4

An Unwanted Dream

In the next couple of days, we searched the library and a couple of shops around the village, hoping to find maps, books, or anything that could help us find some answers. But to no avail. I visited Mr. and Mrs. Malik to see what information he could give, but he suggested that I drop the matter and leave well enough alone before someone else gets hurt. We were frustrated, me more so than the rest. I felt so connected to all of this, but now the answers seemed so far away that the whole thing felt hopeless. The man in the woods, the unicorns, and the melancholy state that I often feel. I couldn't help but feel that it was all connected somehow. So, I decided to walk back to Ms. Crosman's. I didn't want to bother her anymore, especially on this matter because of what she'd been through, but she was my last resort, and I was desperate for help. I knocked loudly at her door, and immediately she answered.

"Hello, Torren. What brings you back?"

"Good afternoon, Ma'am. Do you have a moment?" I asked.

"Yes, I believe I do. Come in. Would you like a piece of briskberry scone?"

"Yes, please. That sounds lovely." She handed me a scone and a cup of coffee.

"I guess everyone knows how much I love coffee," I chuckled.

"It's definitely not a secret. You have coffee everywhere you go, so I'm told."

"Told? I didn't think—why would you be asking others about me?"

"That is a great question. Since your visit the other day, I've been bothered by the events you and your friends have been through, especially when the High Elf said that cursed unicorns were myths, along with black magic. It hurts to know that the ruler of our kingdom would tell such lies. Especially when his father had served in the war. He should know better. It only makes me think that there are secrets behind the walls of Eru Psyawla. Possibly a reason why Mr. Malik was captured."

"I've had the same feeling. But why the secrecy? Wouldn't that cause more harm to the kingdom?"

"One would think, Torren. But we won't know until those secrets are uncovered."

"We need to find books, or something, from the wartime. Those would have documented the events that occurred during the war. The answers should be there," I suggested.

"And then what? March into Eru Psy and shove them in the of the Council? Like here, these papers explain that you're wrong and I'm right. Like that would get you killed?" Ms. Crosman laughed as if she was amused at the thought.

"Well, I mean, kind of was the plan. Maybe not as aggressively, but sure. It's the only plan I have for now."

"Torren, I am willing to help you, but not if you're going to be reckless. You need a solid plan. It doesn't have to be perfect, just carefully thought through."

"I understand."

"Let me see what I can find. It's a cluttered mess in here, so it may take some time to find anything useful. Come back in a couple of days, and hopefully, I'll have something for you," Ms. Crosman explained as she sipped on her cup of coffee. "And hopefully, by then, you and your friends can draw up a solid plan."

"Thank you," I said cheerfully as I stood up to take my empty cup to the kitchen. I washed the coffee cup and put it in the cupboard for Ms. Crosman. "You didn't have to do that; I would've gotten it later on."

"It's no problem, Ms. Crosman. I don't mind."

"I guess I better get looking. I'll see you in a couple of days," Ms. Crosman sighed as I walked out through the door.

I left Ms. Crossman's house and started heading home when I heard an echo of neighs come from the edge of the wood next to her house. As I looked, the melancholy feeling I had felt a few days ago returned. This time, with vengeance. I could barely breathe. I fell to my knees and cried uncontrollably.

"What is this?!" I shouted. "Why do I hurt so badly?"

Then, suddenly, a flash of images streamed in my mind, but as if they were right in front of me. I could feel their presence surrounding me. A black unicorn, with eyes as dark as the night without the stars or moon shining and blood on its horn, stood atop what seemed to be a dead unicorn. Riding the evil creature was a man wearing a black cloak embellished with red and purple streaming down the sides and lacing at the bottom. His presence was cold as winter and empty as a black hole. I felt scared, frozen in time. Petrified. I couldn't scream or move, which frightened me more. The two images seemed to walk closer to me and abruptly appeared right over me. The man in the black cloak was holding a crown just like the one the High Elf wears, and it burst into flames. Suddenly, a flash of light and the man and the black unicorn were gone, and two normal, seemingly young unicorns were right next to me.

A voice echoed, "Forgive, but do not forget. Cure the dark, but do not blind with light. Save us all." An elf appeared, wearing a white cloak laced with orange and green embellishments, and stood over me. I didn't recognize her or the voice. I still couldn't speak. And then she pointed, and everything went black.

I awoke in Miri's house, confused and panicky. My vision was blurred, and the sounds around me were muffled. I was terrified. I sat up in a frenzy, swinging my arms wildly and screaming, "Where am I?! What happened?!" and things of that sort.

"Calm down, it's okay. You're safe," Miri stated calmly while placing a hand on my back. "You're at my place. Here, take a drink of water."

I took a long drink, placed the cup on the table, and muttered, "Thank you. Can I have some coffee, please?"

"Sure," Miri laughed.

"Do you remember what happened?" Cormac asked.

"I—I...I'm not sure," I replied shakily. "It was terrifying...and weird. I couldn't move or speak," I explained with a tremble in my voice. Over the next few moments, I explained what I saw and the voice that still echoed. As terrifying as it was, it was still beautiful. Soft.

"Well, what does that all mean?" Kyna asked, obviously freaked.

"I think we're in over our heads with this, guys. I mean curses, black magic, strange visions. Maybe we should explain to the High Elf and the Council," Cormac suggested.

"No. We can't. It's obvious that they are hiding something," Kyna strongly suggested.

"Which is one reason why we can't go to them and why we must uncover the truth. No matter how crazy it sounds, how stupid it might be, we have to figure out what all this means," Miri stated, turning her head toward me as if she were reading my mind. "How do you feel, Torren?" Miri asked softly.

"I'm okay. Hungry though. What is there to eat?"

"I'll get you something. Hold tight."

As Miri went to get me food from the kitchen, there was a knock at the door.

"Ms. Crosman. Mr. Malik. Come in," Aevin stuttered as he opened the door, shocked.

"Thank you. We heard what happened. The entire village is talking about it. Torren, are you okay?" Ms. Crosman rambled as she stepped inside.

"I'm fine, thank you."

"So," Ms. Crosman pulled a book from her bag and a few other miscellaneous documents. "These should be useful. Granted, some are in pretty bad shape. This book tells the history of Eru Psyawla before and after the war. I read through it a bit last night, and it's very intriguing. All sorts of magic and curses. Though, there a particular section that had been ripped out."

"Must be important," Lorcan said. As we sat and looked through the books and items that Ms. Crosman had brought, my mind wandered. That voice. It seemed familiar, but not at the same time. Who were they? Did I know them? Do they know me? Who am I supposed to help, and how? I wasn't sure what we were supposed to do, no one was.

"Well, I think Torren still needs to rest," Miri suggested.

"Yeah, I think you're right. Thank you all for coming. And thanks, Anglin, Ms. Crosman, for the books."

Dusk awaited a new sense, a new feeling. I knew what we had to do, but no idea how to accomplish it. We had to find the cursed unicorn and figure out a way to save it, if it wasn't too late. Find a way to expose the lies the Council and High Elf have spread in order to cover their secret and find out what that secret was. What would they want to keep from the citizens of the kingdom? I sat up in the bed that Miri and the others had made for me in the living room during my unwanted and untimely sleep. Out the window, you could see the birds sitting in the trees, singing their songs to one another, beautifully echoing through the village. It gave me a sense of peace and calm. Miri walked into the room from the kitchen carrying a tray of fruit and bread with sweet mixberry spread.

"Good morning, sleepy head," Miri joked while placing the tray on the table next to me. She had a smile on her face, her hair was braided in a weave of beautiful waves flowing on top of silk, beautiful and smooth. Soothing. Made the mood this morning filled with an even more relaxing presence. She was a great person. Kindhearted, loving, passionate. Beautiful.

"Thank you, Miri."

"So. What do we do about all this…mystery within the kingdom?"

"We need to go through the texts and see what they say. Hopefully, we will know what to do after. I'll take a book; you and the others distribute the other books and go through them. The answers have to be in one of them."

We visited the others, handing them a book or stack of papers to scan through. Most of the books didn't mention anything useful, unless you wanted old recipes on how to cook insects, or how the town of VaHaile was built. Interesting, but not very helpful when trying to find information on cursed unicorns.

"Miri, why do you think Mr. Malik refuses to talk about his endeavors in the forest?"

"I keep wondering the same thing. He's either protecting himself or trying to protect us."

"Or it could be both," I implied. "There is nothing helpful in my book. Anywhere. It's the *History of VaHaile, a New Home*."

"Yeah, mine isn't much help, either. Insects and animals of the Forest," Miri stated in a joking voice. We laid the books on the table next to us and just sat for a bit. Enjoying each other's company and the silence that surrounded us. Today had been the most peaceful of the last several days. It was refreshing. Energizing. It was what we needed, more than answers, at that moment. We spent most of the day playing Stones and Sticks and cleaning her house a bit. After dinner, we decided it would be a great idea to meet up with the others for a game of Shadow Hunter. Lorcan was helping his parents repair a broken fencing that was damaged by the goats they raised. More trouble than they're worth most of the time, if you ask me. But they do provide some good milk, that's for sure. The rest of the cousins and Cormac were thrilled to be able to join. We didn't talk about any type of adventure or curse other than who was going to be the "shadows" and who would play the "hunter" first. Of course, I was chosen to play the hunter to start the game, which is better than Kyna being a hunter. She's so stealthy and witty with tracking down the shadows, the game only lasts a couple of minutes. It's her favorite game, after all. Surprisingly, I found all the shadows within just a few minutes. Beating my old record of twenty-four minutes. We took turns going back and forth between the two sides, not realizing how late it had gotten. One of the Rangers babysitting us came over and announced that the other villagers would like to sleep, so we had to call it a night. But it was what we all needed, to take our minds away and not think for a moment.

I was sitting down to eat my lunch the next day when the cousins, Miri, and Ms. Crosman burst through my door like wildfire chased them inside.

"Torren! Torren! You won't believe what I—we found!" Aevin shouted as he ran toward me, jumping over my coffee table.

"This book was a disguise. It talks about the war, but not the real war. It's how they want us and the future generations to see the war," Ms. Crosman added. "It's the real reason I was let go from teaching."

"Well, what do you mean, exactly? That it was a disguise?" I asked, confused.

"Well, I was reading through the book, finding useless information, obvious lies, boring storing, and then exciting tales of battle."

"Aevin, get to the point, man," I interrupted.

"Sorry. Anyways. I was reading, and I accidentally knocked over my lantern onto the paper I was reading, and it caught fire. The closest thing to me was my cup of mushroom coffee, so I doused the flame with it; it smoked this purple and red color, and when I saw the pages, they looked completely unharmed. I noticed the paragraphs looked different, so I started reading them again, and they were changed! I read again from the beginning, and it was like reading a completely different book!"

"That's because it was enchanted with a spell to mask the true writing of the book. Which, in turn, helped the book keep its crisp, new form. And smell, I do love the smell of a freshly made book," Ms. Crosman informed us.

"Who and why would someone do that?" I asked.

"I have a feeling the answer to that may lead to more than just answers," Ms. Crosman pointed out. And she was most likely speaking of death, or at least dangers. We all could feel it. A sense of doubt and fear filled the air while we sat in silence, contemplating the outcomes, good and bad. We knew going to Eru Psyawla and exposing the truth would mean imprisonment, if not death. Add in hunting down a cursed unicorn and the man who trapped Mr. Malik; it didn't look good for us.

"I know that we've spoken about it, thought about it, and everything else, but now we have something to go on. We're all scared, but aren't you also scared of why they have these secrets? And I guarantee it's all connected: the unicorn, the man in the words, Torren's dream, vision, or whatever it was, the lies of Eru Psy royals. It has to be connected," Miri stated strongly.

"Hey, look! What is that?" Cormac muttered while hunching closer to the book he was looking through. There was a very vague color difference on the corner of the cover, which had slightly been pulled up. But the color didn't seem to be caused by fading or being tugged over the years. More like it was a different piece of material. We assisted Cormac in pulling the material back, carefully, by instructing him on the best way to pull it back without damaging the book, or so we thought.

"All right, guys. I got it, I got it. Just *shhh*," Cormac insisted while putting his finger to his lips, obviously annoyed with our...bossing. A minute later, he had finally peeled back the material on the cover, and underneath was a picture of a map.

"Is that...Zynthia?" I asked, surprised.

We stared at the map lying across my table for a long while, studying the landmarks and features. The features matched with the kingdom, but there were landmarks that we couldn't recognize. The Aztrean Mountains go up to the north, stretching a few miles west. Eru Psyawla is just southeast of the mountain range. Tenebrae at the south of the Kingdom. And VaHaile to the east of Eru Psy. The rivers flowing on the east and west. But a few miles following the Druslan River, there seemed to be a cave, or some kind of land feature, just past Vondors Point. We couldn't really tell what it was, honestly. But it seemed important because there was a marking next to it, like an asterisk. None of us had ever been there. Sure, we had traveled the river a way, but we never had reason to go to Vondors Point. The terrain that way was treacherous, much too hard for an elf like me to travel for fun. The maps we had used today didn't have the landmark, nor follow the river as far as the map that lay before us.

"This is strange. This landmark isn't on recent maps, or in any of the books. What is it?" Lorcan asked. "I've followed this river many times, hunting and fishing, but I never seen a place near here." He pointed at the landmark on the map.

"Have you followed that far east?" I asked.

"I mean, I've gone pretty far. I lost my bow in the river and tried to retrieve it. Let's just say I went home very angry and wet," Lorcan grumbled. "I remember, vaguely, about a place my father would talk about around that area, but..."

"But nothing in any of these texts about my dream?" I asked, irritated.

"Unfortunately, none that we've found."

"Well, maybe we can explore the mysterious cave, or whatever it is, and find more answers?" Kyna shrugged. We all wanted to go, regardless of how frightened we were. This was bigger than we could have ever imagined. The secrets were buried deeper.

"But what about Mr. Malik? What's his secret?" I asked.

"Every time I try to speak to him about his captor, he brushes it off and demands I leave it alone."

"We will worry about that later. For now, we follow the clues we have," Miri commanded.

"Okay. So, we need to figure a way to leave without the guards noticing," Lorcan said.

"That's easy. What worries me is that they have us check in every day or come knock at our door. How do we deal with that?" I asked.

"We're still confined for a while. They're going to notice if we aren't here."

"Do we chance it?" Cormac asked.

"Not just yet," replied Miri. We stayed in my house, trying to come up with a reliable plan to leave without the guards figuring out that we had left. The truth was, there wasn't a great plan. Nothing. We were stuck between a rock and a hard place. Finally, we decided to really just go for it. We'd have a head start on the guards, especially if we left early in the morning. They wouldn't do a check until the afternoon.

The next day, clouds roamed above, dark and ominous, like it was angry that we planned to leave the village. We didn't know if the landmark led to treasure or death, or maybe it was what the man in the woods was asking Mr. Malik about. But we had to find out. Keela would have to stay back this time as she was still nursing a broken leg. The rest of us packed a small bag with some small snacks, mostly nuts and berries. Some small essential items for making coffee, we all know that is most important. Canteens for water, and what we could carry as a weapon in case we run into danger. We had to pack a light. According to the map, the terrain would be much worse than it was when we went toward Tenebrae.

The only person we talked to about our adventure was Ms. Crosman. She was a bit uneasy about the trip and the risks that may come with it, but was excited to possibly uncover the truth, though not excited enough to join us. However, she would not cover for us if questioned by the guards. I explained to her that I wouldn't expect her to and wouldn't want her to be in any trouble. We started our journey just after midday. The clouds still hung in the sky, big and black, but no rain had fallen yet. Which was good because it would certainly make the journey much more difficult, given the hills we had to climb in the beginning. We certainly didn't want another "Keela" moment. High One forbid another person got hurt that month and it was my fault again. The journey was taking longer than expected. We had already walked a little way past Vondors Point, the area where it stopped on all recently made maps. Still, we had not found the marking we were looking for. The land was of different soil the closer we got. Almost like ash mixed with… tar? It was strange and definitely not a good sign. Fortunately, it was a sign that we could be in the right area.

The sun was starting to set. We were so tired and hungry. We hadn't stopped all day in fear the guards would be chasing behind. We knew it would be a matter of time before they were looking for us. They probably already started. Which didn't leave us much time.

"Guys, we set camp here tonight," Lorcan commanded. "It's as good a place as any."

"We need to disguise ourselves somehow, with branches and leaves or whatnot. We know the guards will be looking, eventually. We can't have them capturing us before we even find the landmark," I pointed out.

"We can take turns keeping watch. I'll take the first watch, Lorcan second watch. Cormac, Torren, Aevin, and then Miri?" Kyna suggested wisely.

"Good idea, Kyna. So, what do we do once we find whatever it is that we are supposed to be finding?" Cormac questioned with a tilt of his head, like he knew no one had been planning ahead. Truth was, we hadn't. It didn't cross any of our minds, not even once. We just didn't want to get caught leaving the village, and then find the landmark and whatever secret it held. We didn't have time to think ahead.

"We will figure that out once we get to that bridge. Or something like that," I remarked, but not very well.

"I believe it's supposed to be 'We will cross that bridge once we come to it,'" Miri corrected while lightly shoving my shoulder.

"Sounds about right; I was close, though," I chuckled. "We better sleep while we can. We need to start early in the morning. Thankfully, I think we're close. Judging by this strange soil we've walked the past mile, we should run into it anytime now," Kyna said hopefully. We were all hopeful. But scared. All sorts of problems lie in front and behind us. But what scared us the most was that of the unknown.

Meanwhile, in Tenebrae, the cursed home of the werewolves, awaited those longing for freedom. The eyes that Torren had felt so strongly in the woods and walking through the village, was a Hexumbra. A Hexumbra, a shadow-like spell that resembles a person, summoned by the Alpha and sorcerer, Jordiah, had relayed information regarding the freelance elves' travel. Now, these hexes, when cast, are only meant to spy. They cannot kill or harm. After all, it is a shadow.

Excited at the news, Jordiah jumped from his chair at his throne and muttered, "It is time." He then walked down the center of the fortress and stood at two big wooden doors.

"Gather to the edge of this cursed land. There, I will lead you to a new home. A better home! One we should have inherited long ago. It is time to take back what is ours!" Jordiah shouted angrily. With the command, the pack marched out of the crumbling stone fortress, through the fog-covered village and broken houses, and through the dying forest.

"Jordiah, we cannot take form for a few nights. And how do you plan to get us out of here?" the Beta, Sabastian, asked.

"Sabastian, you ask too many questions. All in due time, and that time is about to come," Jordiah spoke with promise.

The werewolves made it to the edge of Tenebrae and stopped right where the cursed land began. The pack was eager to start their march outside the curse. To breathe in the fresh air of Zynthia's lush forest and sky. To feel freedom. Few of these wolves were alive during the great war. Most alive today are the children of those who served in the war. Revenge had been a thought festering in their hearts and minds for quite some time. They were impatient.

Jordiah knew the impatience would get them killed, so he instructed: "The path to Eru Psyawla will wait. First, we stop at VaHaile. There is something there that belongs to me. To us! But we must be swift. Smart. And above all, patient. You all have served me well, and for that, I give many thanks. But do not act out of control or foolish. I will not be too kind if this mission were spoiled due to lack of barring."

He then pulled a stone about the size of a plum, purple in color, from his jacket pocket and lifted it in the air. "This stone," he shouted while looking out amongst the crowd, "the Stone of Liber, will allow us to travel beyond this cursed land. There is a problem, however. I can only open a door through the curse for three minutes. After that, the door will seal again, and the stone will turn to dust. Leaving us this one chance to accomplish our lifelong goal. This is the reason I have waited until now to use it. The cloak has been found. With the cloak, all things change. Starting with our home! To VaHaile...we march!"

Jordiah's speech sparked the very souls of his clan as they shouted and cursed the name of Zynthia in unison. Their spirits were lifted for the first time since the great war. Jordiah hushed the rowdy crowd before him, touched the stone to the field that surrounded the village, and spoke these words— *"Aperta Ianua. Transeamus!"* and one by one, the wolves of Tenebrae passed through the door to begin their reign in Zynthia.

Back near Vondors Point, Miri woke us just before dusk. The fog settled close to the ground, laying a blanket of white around us. The forest was filled with ominous images lying behind the white cloud, casting a scene that looked almost like a nightmare.

"You sleep okay? Any wild dreams you'd like to share?" Miri joked as she woke me.

"I slept fine and no dreams, thankfully," I replied.

"Good. I don't know how many more weird events we can handle. You know, I never would've thought I'd be out in the woods, looking for a missing person or secret...whatever it is we're looking for now, especially with you. The worry-wart homebody."

"Yeah. Me neither. But here we are. Surrounded by fog, looking for something that we don't even know what 'it' is. Though, I'm sure we will know once we find it."

"I'd say you're right, Torren," Miri agreed. "Who knows where this thing is, though? We need to look at the map and assess where we are," she stated as she stood up quickly. "Lorcan. Bring the map over here."

Lorcan ruffled through his bag and pulled out the map. Miri and I met him halfway and sat the map on top of an old tree stump to get a better look at it. There wasn't much light still because the sun hadn't risen much, but there was enough light through the trees and our lanterns that we could make out images.

"Okay, here is Vondors Point. We passed it a while back; I remember that small meadow just a few minutes back," Lorcan said.

"Which should put us..." he paused and scanned the map. "Here. We should be right around here." He pointed his finger at a tree line that was right at the mysterious landmark, right next to a big boulder.

"Do you see that boulder anywhere?" I asked while trying to look through the dark and the fog to find it. "According to the map, the boulder should be right over this way." I walked with the lantern toward the direction that correlated with the boulder on the map.

"I don't see it over here!" I shouted.

"Hey, quiet. We don't know if anyone is here looking for us," Miri reminded me. There was that feeling again of loneliness and sadness.

"It's here," I grunted as I walked back to Miri and Lorcan.

"The boulder? Hey. Are you okay?"

"No, Miri. It's the cursed unicorn. I feel it." A neigh echoed just behind us. We looked, half scared and unable to move.

"*Oh*, no." Gasped Kyna as the unicorn came into the light. The creature was a sleek black from hoof to horn. Even its eyes. It seemed dead inside and had a certain hunger in its stare that froze us to our core. Lorcan couldn't even pull back his bow and arrow. The creature let out a whine and stepped forward, bowing its head. I knew it was stupid and crazy, but I had to get closer to it.

"No, Torren. Don't. Just move back. Slowly," she whispered with a tremble in her voice.

"It's okay. It's okay. You guys stay back. I have to do this." I moved closer, slowly, and each step I took, the fear I had melted into sadness, but I kept inching my way. Finally, I was almost arm's length away. The beast reared back on its hind legs and let out a deathly *neeiigghhh* before landing on its two front hooves.

I took a step back and held my hand out. "It's okay. I'm a friend. We all are," I muttered. Suddenly, the unicorn stepped forward and gently lowered its head, allowing my hand to be placed on it. The sadness and despair that was in the unicorn seemed to lift and swirl in the air as a bright light gleamed like a halo around my hand.

"What in the dragon's fire is happening right now?" shouted Cormac. The others stood, shocked, as they watched the sleek black fur of the unicorn fade to white. I fell to my knee moments later, with a tear in my eyes, and I felt freer than I had ever felt in my life. Like a bag full of stone was crushing my back and was finally lifted off. It was amazing.

I looked up at the unicorn and whispered, "Go. Find your foals. They need you." The unicorn, now white with a beautiful set of eyes, looked at me, bowed its head, and ran off into the wood behind it. Miri ran over to me, flabbergasted at what just happened, as we all were.

"Are—are you okay?" She hugged me, squeezing me tighter than she ever had.

"I'm the okayest I've ever been," I replied with a smile on my face. She pulled back, looked at me, and then slapped me right on my face.

"Don't ever do that again, Torren! I—I—I...don't know what we'd do without you," she said, stumbling with her words.

"Does that thing follow you, Torren?" Aevin asked.

"I'm beginning to think it has been," I replied while staring in the direction in which the unicorn had run.

After we all settled out of the frightening event with the unicorn, we decided to look for the mysterious landmark. We split into teams of two, each team covering a different section. We decided we would cover about fifty yards if we could. After searching for a while, a long while, we met back at the campsite.

"Anything?" I sighed.

"No" came from all of them.

"It doesn't make sense. According to the map, it should be right around here. We covered enough ground searching that surely someone must've spotted something," I stated with frustration.

"What has made sense lately? You just found out that you can heal a cursed unicorn, we found a strange map that no one has seen that doesn't correspond with the maps we've seen. Mr. Malik was captured in the middle of the forest outside Tenebrae. Nothing makes sense right now," replied Cormac.

"Yeah, not to mention the lies from the High Elf and his Council," Kyna remarked. We sat quietly for a while, gathering our thoughts and trying to relax. Thankfully, Miri was thoughtful enough to make coffee and breakfast after we all settled down a bit. The sun had been in the sky a while now, so we knew we had to get moving. Enough time had been spent already. We just didn't know where else to look.

"You're it," Miri said as she ran over and tagged me on the shoulder.

"Hey! Wh— Oh, all right," I grunted as I stood up chasing her. She was too far ahead, so I went for Lorcan, who, luckily for me, was standing next to a tree talking to Kyna and not paying attention.

"You're it, Lorcan." I tagged him on the arm and ran back in the opposition direction. He quickly tagged Kyna, who was still processing what was going on.

"*Oh*, come on! I wasn't paying attention, not fair, Lorcan!" she complained, and she stood up, stumbling over a tree root. Miri always knew how to lighten a mood and make us forget about things for a moment. It's what we needed after all of us nearly having a heart attack this morning and struggling to find that landmark. I moved over to the stump that we laid the map on and crouched behind, hoping to escape Kyna's gaze as she went around, trying to tag someone. I got distracted by a bird in the trees above me, and before I knew it, Kyna was running at full speed, about to get me. I dove out of the way just in time, but it caused her to trip over the stump and go flying through the air. Me and Cormac ran over to her to see if she was okay. While we were kneeling beside her, I got a glimpse at the stump. It looked as if it shifted a bit in our direction.

"Odd. Does that stump look different to you?" I pointed to the stump.

"Well, I'm fine, thanks, Torren," Kyna scoffed.

"Sorry, Kyna. I just couldn't help but notice something seemed...off. Can you stand, though?" We helped Kyna to her feet and watched as she moved her leg and bent it to make sure she was all right.

"Yeah, I'm good," she assured us.

As we walked toward the stump, it looked as if it sort of tilted off the ground in which it was before. Standing over top of the stump, we clearly saw that it had moved, but it looked like something underneath the stump. It wasn't earth. I mean, there was dirt over top of whatever it was, but there was a shine to it. Like metal. So, we figured it'd be a good place to look, especially since we've looked everywhere else in the area. We started digging around the stump so we could move it, which took longer than any of us wanted. The roots were deeper than we imagined they'd be, and they seemed to be in better shape than previously thought. After much hard work and lots and lots of soil and dirt, we finally managed to loosen the stump enough to maneuver it out of the way.

"Well, would you look at that?" Lorcan said as he dusted the top. It was a polished stone door, which, unfortunately, was locked.

"How do you think we get in? Do we think this is what we're looking for?" Miri questioned.

CHAPTER 5

The Path to the Truth

The door was locked shut. It seemed there was a key that fitted the lock, but none like we had seen. "Miri, do you think you can use your skills to unlock it?"

"I'm not sure; what if it has some kind of magic spell protecting it?"

"You could try, though, couldn't you?" asked Kyna. Miri grabbed the lock with one hand and stretched out the other hand, moving it as if it were the key. She concentrated deeply for a moment, letting out a few grunts and moans.

"Ahh. Got it," she exclaimed as the lock unhooked.

"Knew you could do it, Mir."

"Thanks, Torren. I've never broken into anything before. It's kind of...a rush." We opened the hatch door, looked inside but it was pretty dark, but we could see the bottom, so we knew it couldn't be too deep. Though traps could still be waiting to go off once we step foot in the unknown.

"Who goes first?" Aevin asked while looking around.

"We don't have time to waste, so I'll go first," Lorcan stated. We handed him a lantern and watched him carefully go down the ladder. "I made it. It looks pretty safe so far," he muttered.

"Looks like it leads out toward that way," he said as he pointed toward Vondors Point.

"Well, let's see what it's in there," I said as I started down to the pit. Aevin was the last of us to climb down. As he was on his way, he did the best he could to pull the stump back to its original place. He didn't quite get it right, but we figured it'd work for now. Our lanterns wouldn't last very long, and we needed them for travel at night on the way back, so we were hoping to be in and out pretty quickly. The path that Lorcan pointed out started going towards Vondors Point, but quickly turned left twice, causing us to go further away from the village and back in the direction of the pit door.

"Seems counterproductive, right?" Cormac pointed out as we started down the second left turn. "Why not just have the path go this way from the start?"

"Who knows, Cormac? Maybe the soil there wasn't able to hold the shape to create the path?" I suggested. The walls were held up with stone and some planks of wood, which were not in the best-looking shape and made me feel even more worried about our situation. We followed the path for moments and made a right turn. At this turn, there were steps leading to a doorway, this one made of wood and thankfully unlocked.

When we opened the door, there was a ledge on our side, followed by a gap that traveled a few meters to another ledge that housed a wooden chest atop a stone dais. We scanned the room, looking for a way across. Below, all you could see was darkness. Thankfully, the ledge seemed sturdy enough to keep us from falling to our deaths.

"What do we do now? Whatever is in that chest has to be what we came for," Kyna remarked.

"I'm not sure. Though, I am certain there is a trap. We have to be careful. Who knows how far that pit goes," I said. "I am surprised, however, that we hadn't run into any danger before now."

"Probably because there's no way to go to the other end, Torren, and they knew that," Cormac said with frustration.

"No, there has to be a way. We just have to look," Miri slapped Cormac on the arm.

"There. What's that over there?" Kyna pointed to a stone on the wall, just to the left of us. It was a different shade than the rest of the stones, only slightly, but there seemed to be a marking on it. Three symbols were marked on the stone.

"It's the ancient language. I recognize it from when my parents taught it to me as a young elf. Now I wish I had paid more attention," Lorcan informed us.

"Well, can you read it?" Kyna asked.

"Let me try. I haven't read the ancient language in a very long time, and usually, it's in word form. These are symbols that represent the word or phrase, whichever it is, and will take more time." We stood behind Lorcan, surely making him nervous as he tried to remember the symbols. He began to mutter phrases and words, "S...site...Sit. Mia. No. That's not right. V—via." He seemed hopeful. "*Sit via apparebit!*" he shouted. Unfortunately, nothing happened.

"What in blazes do we do now? Maybe you said it wrong," Kyna insinuated. Lorcan then pushed the stone into the wall and repeated the words one more time.

"*Sit via apparebit!*" The walls began to shake, and slabs of stone glided from them, lining up perfectly with the two platforms, creating a walkway to the chest.

"*Huh!* So that's how we get across," Cormac chuckled.

"Good job, Lorcan. Thank the High One someone learned the ancient language."

"Thank my parents when we return to the village. It was their idea to teach me and my brothers," Lorcan said. We slowly stepped toward the other side of the stone walkway, being careful to watch for any sort of arrows shooting from the walls or any deathly trap that could be set. Fortunately, there were no traps, and we made it safely to the chest. Slightly surprised that it seemed rather easy. You would think a chest buried underground through a series of tunnels in the middle of the forest would be important enough to have traps or some kind of safeguards in place so that it wouldn't fall into the wrong hands.

"So, do we grab the chest and run, or open and here? What do we do?" I questioned as I looked at each of my friends, trying to find an answer.

"What if we open it, and the ground crumbles beneath us, causing us to tumble to our deaths?" Cormac shared his worries with us.

"What if the same thing happens when we pick up the chest? Can we even lift it?" We all shared our thoughts and argued back and forth about what could happen if we did this or that.

"There. Problem solved," Miri said as she opened the chest. A few of us gasped and looked around frantically, waiting for something to happen, but nothing did.

Feeling relieved that no traps had been set off from opening the chest, we looked inside. There was only a cloak.

"A cloak. A cloak! We risked coming here for a single cloak!" Kyna shouted in anger. "This is ridicu—"

THE KINGDOM OF ZYNTHIA: BLOODLINE

"Wait," I interrupted Kyna's rant. "It can't be," I stuttered as I looked down at the cloak, black with red and purple embellishment, just like the one the dark elf wore in my vision.

"What is it, Torren?"

"Guys, this is the same cloak the elf wore in my vision. It must be important somehow, right?"

"I don't understand why someone would hide a cloak of all things this far in the middle of nowhere," Lorcan said while sitting on the stone platform. Lorcan grabbed the cloak out of the chest, which turned out to be a very bad idea. A chain reaction occurred the second the cloak lifted from the chest floor. First, the stone pathway leading back to the door we came from crumbled into the darkness underneath, and then a stone fell and landed right in front of that same door. The scariest part was when the room around us began to shake. We panicked. We didn't know what to do. There wasn't another way in or out that any of us had seen before, anyway.

"What now?!" Kyna shouted.

"There has to be another way out; there's no way the person who placed the cloak here would want to trap themselves if they ever came back for it," Lorcan pointed out.

Quickly, we gathered ourselves, except for Cormac, who was on his knees, panicking and shouting, "We're goners! We're going to die!"

"That's not helping," I remarked. "Calm down, take some deep breaths. We will find a way out," I comforted Cormac while placing my hand on his shoulder. The ledge we were standing on started to feel smaller and smaller each second, with stone and dust slowly but steadily raining down on us.

Kyna walked over behind the dais that held the chest, studied it, and started pressing the stones on the wall in panic.

"There's no time for games, Kyna," Aevin shouted.

"I'm not playing. I'm looking for a way out. There has to be a secret door, some way out." And she was right. A few short moments later, Kyna must have pressed the right stone because a slab of stone crumbled in the back wall right next to her, creating a doorway. We didn't even examine the room we were entering; we just ran like our lives depended on it, because truthfully, they did. Once we all entered the room, we stood there in shock and terror, thinking about what had just happened. We were frustrated that all of this was for a cloak. A piece of clothing. All sorts of questions floated around our heads, like "Why a cloak? How is this worth someone's life?"

We examined the room after we all caught our breath and dusted off some of the debris from the crumbling room. We noticed this new room was lit with candles. They seemed to be of some sort of magic because the flames were blue and white, definitely not the color of a normal flame.

"This just keeps getting stranger and stranger," I sighed.

"No kidding. But at least the flames aren't red or black," Aevin remarked jokingly. The room was empty other than the candles, but the flames led to a path. We had no choice but to follow it. We couldn't go back the way we had come unless we wanted to be crushed or fall to our death.

"Come on, let's go. Hopefully this leads to home," Lorcan said while walking toward the lit pathway. The walls of the tunnels appeared to be built in the same manner as the tunnels we entered through. This path had no twists and only slight turns, and the magic flames traveled the entire length, which for us was fortunate because our lanterns had run out. We eventually came to a dead end, and above us hung a wooden ladder, much like the one from the beginning. I climbed up first but couldn't see any sort of door to open, and this ladder seemed much longer than the previous one. I kept seeing glimpses of light shining through the wall around me. Suddenly, the sound of birds singing caught my attention. I was able to peek through a tiny hole in the wall where the light was shunning through. I couldn't believe what I was seeing. Treetops and bright blue sky lay behind them. What in the world? How hi— Where did this lead to? *How high did I go?* I looked down slightly, and my friends below me could no longer be seen through the darkness.

"You still down there?" I shouted. A stream of "yes" echoed from below. "Come on up, but I'm not sure how you'll feel about this. I—I think we're climbing the inside of a tree." I couldn't believe what I was saying.

"Really not that strange. Not what I expected, but still not all that strange," Miri stated as she climbed her way to me. Once they made their way to me, I started ascending again, but it was long before I stumbled upon a hinge buried within the wall. It reminded me of a hinge that would attach to a hatch door. I pushed against it, hoping to see light peering through as the top lifted, but the top seemed to catch on to something just a brief moment after I pushed it. There was something holding it shut. I skimmed the wall and used my right hand to search for a notch, a lever, something that would push open the door or at least loosen it. I finally stopped and examined the hinge. It was actually a wooden nail with a loop around it. I pulled and pulled at the nail.

"Torren! Why have we stopped for so long?" cried Kyna.

"Just hold on a minute. Patience, my friend." Eventually, I was able to yank out the nail, and a big square chunk of wood fell slightly toward my face, letting in a ray of sunshine. I took my hand and pulled the top of the wooden piece, uncovering a square opening. Through the opening, you could see a huge tree breach stretching out from underneath.

"I knew it!" I said while awkwardly struggling through the aperture, feeling as though the tree was giving birth to me.

"It's a tree!"

"A tree? You mean this…tunnel is a…a hollowed tree!" Cormac said, confounded.

"Yes, Cormac. You've got to see this!" I shouted with excitement.

I climbed down a branch, making room for my friends to join me outside the tree, and sat down with my back against the tree, dazed at the sight before me. How wonderfully drawn, the flow of green trees cast to the mountains against a blue sky as the sun gleamed a light so powerful it warmed your soul. To the right of the mountains, you see the tiptops of the castle in Eru Psyawla. It was amazing to see the kingdom drawn in with the mountain range and trees brushed along all around. It was the most beautiful thing I'd ever seen. Miri plopped down in front of me and sat with her legs straddling the branch. Now it's the most beautiful sight I've ever seen. I smiled as I looked into her eyes.

"What?" Miri giggled. "Is there tree in my hair?" She grazed her hands through her hair frantically.

"No. No," I laughed. "Nothing's in your hair. It's ju— I don't know," I stumbled on my words. "Just look at this place. Could you imagine that we would ever be here? The journey to get here? I mean, it's crazy. And to think all we found was a cloak. Then we come out of a tunnel in the treetops. To see *all* of this." I extended my hands straight out and swung them slowly out horizontally.

"Yeah. I know what you mean, Torren. It's freeing, sort of."

"I know what you mean. Almost like this was painted just for us to see for all the trouble we endured back there."

"Oh, Torren. It wasn't that bad. No one got hurt, and there really should've been more traps down there." As we sat there in silence after her comment, I couldn't help but think she was right. It was almost too easy. A little mind games and adrenaline rushes and poof, we had what we came for.

"I think we should get going, though, as much as I hate to admit it and as much I hate to leave this…paradise," I stated while staring out into the blissful horizon. We slowly and carefully placed our feet on the branches below while descending from the tree. We must have been in the tunnels longer than we thought because the sun had started to set. We knew walking in the dark of the night wouldn't be the greatest idea, but we had to get home, and fast. The guards would be ready to snatch us immediately after we step foot in the village and transport us to Eru Psyawla to be questioned and probably jailed. How would we explain our disappearance, explain anything? Especially in a way that wouldn't offend the High Elf and his Council.

"So, when are we going to speak about what happened with the unicorn, Torren?" Lorcan asked as we walked through the forest.

"I don't know what happened. Nor how to explain it, really. I just know that it feels...good now. Optimistic, if that makes any sense?"

"It sort of does, but not really," replied Aevin.

"Well, when we get back to the village, we will figure it out. Hopefully," I muttered.

"Wait a minute. Do we know where we are?" We stopped walking, turned and looked at each other with confusion, and then I just sat on the ground in a frustrated plop, which actually kind of hurt my rear a bit.

"Bring the map, Lorcan."

"Yeah," he sighed. "Probably be a good idea." He ruffled through his bag, searching for the map, and quickly moved his hands to his pockets, searching each one frantically. At that moment, Aevin and Cormac plopped on the ground, grabbed a sack of jerky, and began to eat.

"This will be good, huh, Aevin?" Cormac joked.

"I—I can't find it. I don't know what happened to it," he panicked. He then remembered that when the pit started to crumble, he lost his footing and stumbled, causing the map to fall from his bag into the darkness below, never to be seen again.

"*Oh* no. No. No. No. No!" Lorcan shouted in frustration while throwing his hands to his sides.

"What? What is it?" Kyna asked.

"The map fell." There was a long pause. "Into...the pit. When it started to crumble."

"How could you let that happen, Lorcan?!"

"What will we do now? We don't know where we are, and it's getting dark," shouted Cormac.

"Yeah, we will be eaten by some ferocious night predator. Or worse, found by the Rangers," Aevin added.

"I'd rather be eaten." There was a moment of arguing and bickering back and forth, which didn't help our situation at all. We were almost out of food, lost, and most likely wanted fugitives of the Eru Psyawla. Things couldn't be worse. Well, they could be, but at the time, it didn't feel like it.

"Okay. Okay. Guys. Look," I demanded. They all stopped their bickering and blaming Lorcan and stood in silence, staring at me, waiting for me to say something inspirational.

"I don't know what to do either. Yes, we lost the map. Yes, we're almost out of food... Yeah, I don't know where I'm going with this. I just wanted you to stop shouting," I explained. They all began arguing again.

"What I think Torren was trying to say," Miri Interrupted their bickering, "is if we settle down, gather our thoughts, we can figure out how to get home, yeah?" she said while looking at me and placing her hand on my forearm.

"Yeah, yeah. Okay. So. What do we do?"

"We know the mountains are in that direction, and the Eru Psy should be right around there." Lorcan pointed out with a finger. "So, the tree we climbed was in that direction." He pointed behind us.

"We should be right to keep going forward, then?" suggested Kyna.

"Supposedly, yes. It would seem that way," Lorcan added. We followed its lead and headed just east of the mountain range. It was dark. Clouds rolled above us as we hiked the forest and hills, hoping we were going in the right direction. We could barely see anything, and our lanterns had run out of flame back in the tunnels. We obviously didn't plan well enough for night travel and dark secret tunnels.

We finally found our way to Vondors Point, a familiar place, when suddenly we heard the echo of a unicorn squeal in the distance, though it sounded as if it were moving closer.

"That didn't sound good," I muttered, stopping in my tracks to get the location of the creature.

"*Reeeee.*" The sound echoed again, only a lot closer this time. A second later, a unicorn leaped over a thicket of bushes and came to a dead stop. I studied the beautiful creature, realizing that it was the same used-to-be-cursed unicorn that I had magically healed...somehow. It was in distress. A lot of distress. It started jumping back and forth and turning around, letting out whines and squeals alternatively. It remembered we were here. It was trying to get our attention. I inched closer to it, still acting sporadically.

Kyna and Cormac grabbed me back and said, "What are you doing now? You are crazy, aren't you?"

The only thing I could think to say back was, "It's fine," as I gently shoved their hands off of me and walked closer to the crazed unicorn.

"What have you gotten yourself into now, girl?" I called as I kneeled on one knee, holding my hand out. The unicorn calmed a bit and walked slowly toward my hand. It let out a soft "*neigghh*" and brushed her head on my palm. It quickly lifted its head, looked back into the darkened forest, and squealed.

"Is something wrong? You're trying to tell us something is wrong, aren't you?" I whispered. The unicorn stood still, staring at me for a moment, and then lowered its head.

"Show us. Lead the way," I commanded. The unicorn turned and started walking back into the darkness and turned its head back at me, as if it were making sure we were following behind.

"Come on, guys, we got to go," I said as I started walking. "Don't ask; I just know we have to follow her." We followed the unicorn; lucky she knew the way because we couldn't see the path hardly at all. Unfortunately, she was running instead of a slow-paced walk. We used all we had in our tanks, trying to keep up with her.

"Can...she...please...slow down!" Aevin said while gasping.

"Oh, come on. A good run is just what the doctor ordered!" Miri replied. She secretly loved to run and was actually a skilled runner, definitely the most skilled of us.

"Aren't you tired at all, Miri?" I surprisingly said in a coherent sentence. Miri laughed and zoomed past me like an agilic, which was one of the fastest animals living near or in the kingdom. They are quite harmless, perfect for catching smaller, more annoying rodents. They actually made really good pets.

"I don't know where this thing is taking us, but if we don't get there soon, I might die," Aevin struggled to say. We stopped for a brief moment so Aevin and, well, most of us could catch our breath and a drink of water.

"W—What is that...over there, behind the tree line?" asked Kyna, slightly out of breath still.

"No," Lorcan muttered and began sniffing the air. Smoke and flame. The scent Lorcan was smelling...was smoke. And just behind the tree line, we caught a glimpse of light dancing behind the darkness. We were terrified. Our family, our friends, our lives were in that village. We ran as fast as we could, hoping that just maybe they were sending a signal to us through flame or having a barbecue, something other than what we feared deep down. We entered the village through a brush, standing in silence, shocked and not sure what to think.

CHAPTER 6

Trouble Found Us

Disclaimer: *Please be advised that the following chapter contains scenes of violence that involve descriptions of harm and death to both people and animals. Reader discretion is strongly advised.*

The flames danced as if a song were playing just for it. Burning hot and free, the fire spread fast and wild through homes, pastures, and our favorite diners. Villagers were running in sheer fear, trying to avoid the blaze, but to no avail for some. A little girl stood, sobbing, just feet away from a smoldering corpse. Tears filled our eyes as our hearts began to race; we were stunned to our core.

"What do we do?" cried Miri.

"Keela," Kyna muttered as she ran off in the direction of her house. "Keela! Keela!" she cried out.

"I—I..." I tried to speak, but I couldn't think of what to say. We heard people yelling in the distance.

"Come out, come out wherever you are!" The voice sounded familiar, but I couldn't see who the voice belonged to through all the smoke and fire and the crowd of people running into the forest.

"Come on. We need to find our families. Lorcan, go find Kyna and her sister and then meet us back here. I don't know how long, but we will meet back here. We should try to stay together as long as we can. Splitting up is usually what gets you killed," I commanded. Fear was still present, but now I was... angry. I hadn't been this mad in a long time. I think the last time had been when I was young, and Matthias had put hot sauce in my favorite bowl of chocolate pudding. I was so furious that I threw the bowl and splattered the hot sauce mixed pudding in his face, stinging his eyes. I felt bad afterward, and my mother made me do his chores for two days to make up for it. He kind of deserved the hot sauce in his eyes, though.

We shuffled through debris that had already been charred, nearly ash, looking for our families. We found Aevin and Cormac's parents hidden in a secret bunker buried beneath a barn. The two families were neighbors, and Aevin's family always wanted to be prepared for, well, anything. Most of the animals had been slaughtered, but at least their parents were all right. Hopefully, we were all this lucky. It was hard to move around the village; the people who had set the fire were still roaming around, creating panic amongst the people. We passed one of the invaders standing atop a dead Ranger guard, mocking his corpse with curses and jokes. Two other guards were still fighting back against the invaders, who we still couldn't identify, but they were not of the elven race. The voice called out again.

"Someone knows who has my cloak or who went after it. You better speak, or all of you will die!" I spotted the man speaking the words through a pile of debris and brush, and I couldn't believe it. It was the man who trapped Mr. Malik, who he had trapped once again, along with his wife.

They were bound to a stake in the ground and had been beaten pretty good from the looks of them.

"Jordiah, please! Stop this madness. No more people have to die. Please, I beg of you," Mr. Malik cried.

"I told you, old elf, you would pay for not bringing me that which is mine. Say goodbye to your wife." Jordiah lowered the torch slowly toward the bottom of the stake, and the Maliks cried and said goodbye to one another.

Suddenly, a "Wait!" shouted from behind Jordiah, who turned in surprise. "What do you want, peasant?" Jordiah growled. It was Ms. Crosman.

"I know who went for the cloak. They should be back anytime now; just don't hurt anyone else."

"Give me a name, woman."

"I—I," Ms. Crosman stumbled and began to sob.

"A. Name. *Now!*" he commanded intensely.

"I...can't. Please. You don't need a name. I know they'll be back soon. But I'm sur—" Jordiah quickly took his blade from his waist and drove it through Ms. Crosman, causing her to let out a small grunt. A tear fell from her cheek as she looked down at the blade impaled in her chest. Filled with rage, I jumped up and began to run toward Jordiah as my friends reached to pull me back, whispering, "No, don't do it!" I was so blinded by hate at the moment I didn't care what they were saying or what danger I may be getting into. I got just meters away from Jordiah, held my arm out, and a beam of light gleamed from my palm, blinding him and his counterparts. Noticing they were stunned, and for a moment I was, too, I raced to untie the Maliks and ran back to grab Ms. Crosman.

Jordiah then muttered, "You. You have no idea what or who I am." As he and his henchmen began gaining sight and sense of the situation, Miri and the others ran to my side.

"You have my cloak, don't you?" Jordiah questioned. "I sense it. You can't hide it from me."

"We don't know what you're talking about," Aevin said, falling, and with just as great timing as ever, the cloak fell from his bag and lay on the ground.

"Aevin, you clumsy—"

"I told you. You can't hide it from me. Bring it to me. Or you all die. I don't care if you're a healer or not," Jordiah interrupted Cormac. I, on the other hand, stood confused by his words. What's he talking about? A healer? Does he know about the unicorn? And as he spoke, he turned his head back to his men, and I noticed something odd. He, too, had pointed ears. Like an elf! His men had more rounded ears, definitely not of the elven race. He also seemed less hairy than the others.

"No," I said sternly, declining his offer for the cloak. Jordiah stepped toward me, and his men followed. The look of hunger was in his red-and-purple-shaded eyes.

"You will die a slo—" Jordiah and his men were tackled to the ground in a surprise attack.

"Run!" a Ranger yelled while fighting the invaders. Jordiah was able to throw a Ranger off of him and dived for the cloak just as Aevin was grabbing it to put back in his bag. Jordiah shoved Aevin while diving and managed to get his dirty hands on the cloak. I dove on Jordiah, fighting to get it back, but he was too strong. He managed to reach his leg up and kick me off, and immediately, a guard jumped on him, punching him in the face, and yelled at us to run. My friends picked me up.

"Forget it, we have to go," Miri said. She pulled me along, leaving behind what may be the very thing that would change everyone and everything in Zynthia...forever.

We went back to our meeting spot and were thankful that Lorcan, Keela, and Kyna were waiting in some bushes. This area of the village seemed to have been forgotten, as it was silent and filled with smoke. Jordiah and his men must have gotten all they wanted from this part. It was gloomy, cloudy, and reeked with death and burnt homes. The fires had started dying down, leaving a trail of ash and despair for all of us to remember. It was a very sad and mournful night. Cries of children and adults rang through the air like a sorrow-filled song, and sights of our worst nightmares lay before us.

"Mr. and Ms. Malik! Are you okay?" asked Keela as we approached them.

"Thanks to your friends, again, I am," he replied.

"Ms. Crosman!" Kyna gasped. "What happened?"

"She was stabbed by an invader," I explained while laying her on the ground.

"Ms. Crosman! Ms. Crosman!" I shouted while shaking her. She moaned something, but we couldn't make out what she said. Miri put pressure on the wound, trying to stop the bleeding. Ms. Crosman began to breathe faster, and her hands were feeling cold. She reached for my face and smiled just before her breathing stopped.

"No. No. No!" I grunted.

"I know," Mrs. Malik said. "But we must mourn later; sadly, there's no time right now," she said as she fought back tears. I looked at Mr. Malik in anger, feeling like this whole situation was his fault. As if he hadn't been in the woods that day, we saved him, none of us would be in this mess and our village wouldn't be ash.

"Those who were fortunate enough to escape went to a place that you won't find on *any* map. I'll show you the way, but we must be sure that none of those mangy mutts follows us," Mr. Malik stated, making sure to add emphasis on "mangy mutts." We followed Ren along the outskirts of the village until we came to a tree, similar to the one we ended up climbing inside of after we found the cloak.

"A redwood tree. One of the largest species of trees you'll find in the forest, though they are sort of rare until you go further north. They grow better there. Anywho, if you found the cloak, you know these trees were used for more than just climbing or to make a bird's home." He seemed happy to finally be able to explain.

"Tunnels," Kyna answered.

"Yes. Long ago. We found that these trees could be hollowed out and were perfect size, usually, to fit elves up or down safely, and left no trace of tunnels underneath. And the scent from its secretions were strong enough to hide our scent from the wolves," Mr. Malik informed us.

"And why are we just now figuring this out?" I asked, angered at the fact there were more secrets in our kingdom.

"The High Elf and the Council believed it would be best if only a few residents knew about the tunnels in case things went wrong and people were captured and questioned by our enemy," Mrs. Malik stated. "It was the best way to ensure the safety of our people as a whole."

"Yes, but in the last couple of weeks or more, there have been too many secrets. I'm just trying to make sense of all this, is all," I said. "It seems most of the fighting and commotion in town have settled down. They'll be looking for us soon. We must hurry." With that said, we quickly climbed halfway up the tree, found the hatch that led to the inside, and climbed in and down into a tunnel.

It was lit the same way as the tunnel we traveled earlier, with blue and white flames, though the area was more spacious here.

"Just up ahead is what we call the safe hole. A place big enough for most of the villagers, which, let's be honest, there aren't a lot of people who live in our village," Mr. Malik informed us as he led through the tunnel. We came to a room that housed many of the residents from VaHaile. Women, children, men, everyone was crying, mourning those we lost to the invaders. The homes that were torched. I scanned the room, frantically looking for my parents among the crowd. I finally spotted them in the far back of the room, near a door.

"Mom! Dad!" I shouted as I pushed through the crowd.

"Torren, are you all right?" my mother, Ailbhe, asked, cheerful to see me alive. "Is that your blood? Are you hurt?"

"It's not mine," I said while looking at the stains on my palm and shirt. It's Ms. Crosman's. She didn't make it," I said sadly. "I'm shaken and angry, but I'm all right."

"Where have you been? When everything started, we searched everywhere for you. You were confined to the village.

There's no way you were in the village. We would have spotted you somewhere," my father, Cillian, said with irritation in his voice.

"Look, we will talk about that later. I need to get back to my friends. There's more going on than you know. You two need to stay here, where it's safe," I commanded.

"Torren, we know more than you think. You don't want any part of it. Trust me," my mom said.

"W—what do you mean? How...Do you know what secrets have been kept?" I couldn't seem to find the right questions to ask because I had so many.

I felt my mother's heart melt from the look in her eyes as she said, "We know everything." How could my parents know what was going on and not speak to me about it? Were they trying to protect me as well? Or were they ordered to be quiet? I needed to find the truth.

"Mom, Dad. If you know something, tell me what to do. And tell me how you know," I tried to say calmly.

"Torren, we can't explain everything to you. You must go to Eru Psyawla and bring your concerns to the High Elf and his Council. And don't speak of it to anyone here, but have you found the light?" she whispered. The light? Was she talking about how I healed the unicorn and how I blinded Jordiah?

"I—I think so. But...I don't know how to make sense of it. Wait...How do you know about...this...light?" I was half confused and half frustrated at my mother's statement and question.

"Just speak with the Council. Tell them everything. Don't take 'no' for an answer," she demanded.

"Mom, I don't understand. What aren't you telling me?"

"Torren, listen. I shouldn't be telling you any of this. It could get me and your father killed. I guess if you're experiencing the gift, with everything going on, it doesn't much matter, anyhow. Tell me, did you find the cloak of ash?"

"Cloak of ash?"

"Yes, black with purple and red stitches along the bottom in a pretty pattern, reaching up the sides?"

"Yes. But..." I hesitated and gave a look of disappointment. "But the invaders got it."

"Oh, No. No. No. No," My mother panicked. "Okay. You must go to the mountain. The Aztrean Mountain. Follow this path." She pointed to the door just to her left in the back of the room. "You'll come to a fork. One goes right. The other goes left. Choose the path on the left. It will lead to a cave just outside the mountain. There, you'll find a path leading to a secret passage within the mountain. You'll know when you see it. If you encounter a dragon, tell them you are my son. They will help you," my mother instructed with a serious tone. I wanted to stay and talk more. There were so many questions I still had, though the haste in her voice suggested that we could not afford the delay. I hugged my parents and wished them goodbye, hoping to see them well when this was all finished.

I searched the room for my friends, meeting with Miri and Cormac first. Their parents seemed to be dealing well, though upset, like everyone else, about the destruction of the village. I explained briefly the instructions my parents gave as we gathered the others. When we reached the twins, we sort of stalled a bit, giving me time to think of a way to have Keela join us.

She was still hurt, but I could tell she wanted to join in on the adventure this time. I couldn't help but feel we would need all the help we could get, but I was tired of secrets and surprising twists, so I couldn't trust asking someone else to come along other than those who I had started this quest with.

"Keela, I'm still worried about your injuries, but I want to try something, but not here. It needs to be in a place that only we," I looked at each of my friends, "can see. Who knows the commotion and attention it would bring if I were to try in this crowded room? Not to mention if something goes wrong," I finished.

"You mean, you want to try to heal me, Torren?" Keela whispered with glee.

"Shh. Shh. Quiet. But yes," I replied. "We need you with us. Plus, I'm sure you'd be more than happy to get rid of that crutch."

Keela chuckled. "Would I ever!"

We ate some rations, secretly packed some bags, and headed toward the door. When we approached the door, I looked back at my parents and gave a nod. My mother nodded back and looked back at the crowd as if we had shared a mind for the moment. We needed a distraction so no one saw us pass through the door, and my mother, the improviser she was, quickly gained the attention of the crowd.

"Everyone! Everyone, listen!" and then she let out a whistle loud enough to wake the dead. "Hey! I have something to say." The crowd turned toward her as she walked to the front of the room. Once the people were all facing my mother, she looked at me, gave me a subtle nod, and began a speech as we quietly passed through the door to the next passage.

Much like the passage before, the tunnel was lit with blue and white flames and seemed well supported on the sides.

"So, does anyone know who invaded our village?" Lorcan asked.

"Werewolves, of course," Cormac replied. "It had to be. The feud and hatred they have toward the elves is well known by everyone."

"I'm not entirely sure, Cormac. The man who seemed to be the leader had the features of an elf. Jordiah, I believe Mr. Malik called him. It doesn't quite make sense, though," I scratched my head, thinking back. "Why would an elf attack their own people? I mean, none of them looked familiar, though; Jordiah was the man who captured Ren in the woods. Other than that instance, I don't know who he is or where he resides."

"I'm telling you, it's werewolves!" Cormac reiterated.

"The others with Jordiah had rounded ears, and tons of hair. So it would make sense. They can't change form at will, but they still have a fighting spirit, ruthless to the bone, and strength beyond natural," I mentioned.

"Still raises the question, why would an elf be taking sides with werewolves?" Aevin asked.

"That's what I'm hoping to figure out," I stated.

"Right here should be good, Keela." We stopped after walking for a brief moment. "I don't want you having to travel too far with that gimp leg of yours."

"Broken. It's a broken leg, Torren. Saying gimp makes it sound...diseased...or something. Whatever, I don't like the sound of it," Kyna growled.

"Oh. I'm sorry, I was just trying to...joke a bit, I guess? I couldn't find a way to phrase what I meant by my comment, but I certainly didn't mean any harm. Kyna and Lorcan helped lay Keela on the ground as I prepared my thoughts on how to access my new gift.

"Ready?"

"Sure am," Keela replied.

"Everyone, keep a distance. I'm really not sure what I'm doing, but...here it goes," I muttered.

"Wait...so, you don't know how to use your power?"

"Keela, I've only had it two days max. Other than the unicorn and blinding Jordiah, I've never used this gift. Just...work with me here, okay?" I said while placing my hand on Keela's broken leg.

"*Oooo*," she grunted.

"Sorry. I'll try to be more gentle."

"You better not kill my sister, or you'll answer to me and Lorcan, Torren."

"And Lorcan?" Miri asked. "Does that mea—"

"Everyone quiet, please. I need to concentrate," I interrupted Miri's question. True, I did need to concentrate, but I also wasn't in the mood for a possible relationship conversation. I closed my eyes and imagined the broken bone inside Keela's, focusing on how the pieces fit. After a short time, my hand began to glow, and a stream of *"Aah"* and other curses came from Keela's mouth.

It wasn't long and Keela exclaimed, joyful "Hey! I think—I think it's better!" She jumped up, and bent both legs, squatting to the ground and back up in a vertical leap, and landed on both feet gleaming with laughter. "Thank you, thank you, thank you! Oh, this is amazing! Torren, you're a healer!"

"I guess I am. I guess I am," I sighed, relieved it actually worked. Also, in shock that I had a gift, a power, but I couldn't understand why I was just now developing it.

"Okay, since you've tested your new and improved leg, I say we get moving. Jordiah and his people are probably heading to Eru Psyawla. Whatever your mother wants us to find must be helpful in some way, Torren. One question, along with many others that I won't mention right now, do you know what it is?" Miri asked.

"Mother said I'd know when I see it. And whatever it is, it seemed pretty important."

The hike through the tunnels was more challenging than we expected. Instead of a mostly flat surface to walk on, the ground elevated in some areas and was filled with tight, narrow passages every little bit. Finally, we came to the fork my mother told me about. Two doors, exactly the same, one on the left and one on the right.

"If one leads to the mountains, the other must lead to...?" Aevin hesitated, waiting for one of us to answer. Apparently, we were not witted enough for Aevin because after a very brief pause, he shouted, "Eru Psyawla!"

"You're right. Well, it's the only thing that makes sense, really. Unless it's another secret place that none of us know about," Miri replied.

"I say we split up and one group checks this passage, while the other takes the path to the mountains," Lorcan suggested.

"I mean, maybe that's a good idea. That way, we can warn Eru Psyawla if this Jordiah guy hasn't already made it there and if that is where this path leads. On the other hand, splitting up usually doesn't end well for one group," I said indecisively as I looked back and forth at both doors.

"I think Lorcan is right. We should split up. Me, Torren, and Cormac will go to the mountain. Keela, Kyna, Aevin, and Lorcan will go to...wherever this other door leads. If you run into trouble, meet back here. If one group circles here and the other group doesn't make it back within..." Miri paused for a moment, thinking of a suitable period of time. "At some point, I don't know how much time, just trust your instinct. If the other group hasn't made it back, the first group searches for them? Or continues on without?" She left it to a vote, and unanimously, we voted to search for the missing group, if it came to that.

"If you run into trouble, mostly Jordiah, try to make your way back here or find refuge in the castle. Whatever you do, do not lead them back to the rest of the villagers," I commanded.

"Don't get eaten by a dragon, guys," Lorcan joked.

"We'll try not to," Miri chuckled back at the effort to lighten the mood. In all seriousness, he meant for us to really not get eaten. Even though the laughter behind it was more playful, we were all terrified to find out what was on the other side of the doors. One led to majestic, giant creatures that could swallow an elf whole or burn them to a crisp with one breath. The other door led to the unknown, though most likely to Eru Psyawla, which we all knew Jordiah would be heading. If the second door did lead to Eru Psyawla, hopefully, they could be warned in enough time. We gathered our things, said goodbye, and passed through the doors, each group of friends not knowing if they'd ever see each other again.

Meanwhile, the invaders were still searching the scorched village of VaHaile.

"Sir, is that the cloak you spoke about?" Sabastian asked.

"Yes, and with it, I can make us shift at will. No more waiting for full moons. Though, there is a second cloak. Legend has it that long ago, my mother and her sister were traveling along an unknown path leading to a cave. Within the cave they found an orb, said to have been gleaming with power. The sisters could feel the power within the orb and began squabbling over it, like siblings would. They ended up dropping the orb, and once it hit the ground, a surge of energy flowed from the orb and embedded amongst the cloaks the sisters were wearing. The sisters were healers, holding powers of light and love. The power from the orb enhanced those powers. This is one of those cloaks. For me, I should be able to produce enough magic to help us shift when we want," Jordiah explained, gazing at the cloak in his hand.

"Among other useful things. My mother's power was given to me, including hatred. The elven race shall pay for what they did to my family. My brothers and sisters."

"But those from the war weren't related to you. Maybe a couple, but they weren't your brothers and sisters."

"Fool, not biological. It's a phrase; in a way, they were all our brothers and sisters."

"So, how do you know that the cloak will allow us to change form at will?" Sabastian asked.

"Because my mother wrote about it, remember? You don't pay attention to anything you're taught, do you? Go. Get out of here before I break your legs," Jordiah commanded with frustration.

"Yes, sir," Sabastian muttered.

"One more thing," Jordiah gave Sabastian an evil stay.

Sabastian gulped, "How do you know what the bother cloak will do?"

"Sabastian, must you ask so many annoying questions?" the Alpha grunted. "Both cloaks hold the greatest power anyone has ever seen. If you put them both together, all that power in one place, one could do an unlimited number of things: curses, destruction. We must find the other cloak."

"What do you plan to do once you have both?"

"Control the dragons and make them destroy the race they love so much, and then..." Jordiah paused. "Kill each other, slowly, so that we, the rightful people, shall inhabit Zynthia. Becoming the dominant species in all the land." Jordiah laughed manically, and Sabastian echoed the laughter nervously.

"Now go and prepare the others. Tonight, we march to Eru Psyawla," Jordiah growled. Sabastian ran to the crowd still standing and scavenging through rubble and those who were unfortunately slain. They did, however, keep some of the elves alive.

"Sir, what shall we do with them?" Liz shouted, standing next to a group of elves bound to the ground.

Jordiah walked over and said, "They could be useful later on in our journey. Perhaps we make them slaves once we take over Zynthia."

"Fine plan, sir. I like it." Liz smiled while staring down at the wounded. The invaders, led by Jordiah, began their march to Zynthia as the sun set among the burning village. Smoke still filled the air around VaHaile, with no hope ahead for those who were captured.

In the tunnels, Cormac, Miri, and I were exhausted, hungry, and sore. The path had a slight incline but wasn't too terrible to hike. Though, all the recent travel, plus walking uphill, in a dimly lit tunnel, was not what our legs ordered. We had not eaten in ages, it felt like. Thankfully, Cormac had a sack of bread and berries left for us to munch on, though, it wasn't all that filling.

"We need to rest, Torren."

"Mir, we will once we find what we're looking for. It shouldn't take that long," I said, trying to make her feel better.

"You don't even know what we are looking for. We haven't slept or had a decent meal in forever," Cormac complained. He was right. It had been a long while since we could actually relax. Though, we should consider ourselves lucky to be alive.

"How do you suppose the others are doing?" Miri asked.

"Lorcan and Kyna are strong and willful. They'll keep the others in line and safe. Aevin can cook anything, and Keela... well, she's...Keela," I explained.

"You know Keela and Lorcan have a thing, right?" Miri whispered, smiling at the thought of love.

"A thing?" I asked, oblivious to what she was suggesting, as I usually was.

"Yeah. A thing. You know. They both like each other, they're just afraid to tell one another."

"Oh, you're full of it, Miri. Don't kid yourself."

"Torren, you can't tell me that you wouldn't be happy for them to, you know, be a couple. It's sweet, I think."

"I can't imagine anyone finding love right now. There's too much going on, and it's too dangerous to think about love and babies right now."

"Oh," Miri muttered and lowered her head.

"What?" I asked.

"Oh, it's nothing," Miri sighed.

"Guys!" Cormac shouted from behind.

"Slow down a bit. I'm getting tired. Just stop a bit. Just for a moment, would ya."

Miri and I stopped and looked back with a mild disgust.

"Cormac, you need to work out a bit more. Build your endurance," Miri laughed.

"We can't all be marathon runners like you, Miri," I joked while poking Miri on the shoulder.

"Ow. That actually hurt a little."

"Sorry, poked harder than I meant, I guess." Out of nowhere, a cool breeze flowed through the tunnel, making the hair on our necks stand erect. There was a slight glimpse of light shining ahead, but it quickly faded.

"What was that?" Cormac's voice shook.

"I don't know. But we can't stop."

"You can't. But I can, Torren."

"Stop being so scared, Cormac. It could be nothing." Miri's voice cracked from fear. "We're all scared, but trust me, we have to move."

We inched slowly forward as the breeze got stronger and colder. We were filled with dread, down to our bones, as we turned the corner. A hole. Something or someone had fractured the wall, creating a window of sorts. I peered out the hole in the mountainside. You could see Eru Psyawla. It was far away, looking small in the distance, but you could clearly see the castle and the surrounding buildings with trees planted behind. We were more than halfway up the mountain. One wrong move, and we would be gone, pancaked on the ground. I began to sweat as my heart pounded.

Miri grabbed my hand and gently guided me back. "Torren, watch your step. You're making me nervous."

We heard a loud scoff, and the breeze became stronger. Shockingly, A dragon swooped down and covered the view from outside the hole, looking straight at us. We froze, gripping the wall behind us. The dragon's face was fierce, but it didn't seem angry. It had a white diamond in the center of its forehead with a blue lightning bolt. The beast was covered in scales and had spikes protruding from the side of its head to the top. It was green in color and had blue eyes, like the color of the sky.

"My name is Zax, guardian of these mountains. What business do you have being here?" The dragon used telepathy to speak to us. It was magical but frightening just the same. Miri jabbed me with her elbow and looked at me as if she wanted me to speak, but I couldn't. I was petrified. I tried to speak, but no words came out.

"I...Tofn...uhh, umm...mm." Gibberish is all that would come out.

"What was that?" Miri whispered.

"Boy, I will not hurt you and your friends; I smell no evil in your blood. What brings you to this mountain?" The dragon's voice in my mind was soft-spoken but stern. Sir...dragon... dragon sir."

"Just Zax will do," the dragon interrupted. "But I applaud your try."

"Zax, I am Torren. This is Miri and Cormac," I said nervously. The dragon inched its face closer, stretching its nose through the hole.

"A Luxmin. I know your smell."

"H—how...how do you know my name?"

"Tell me, is your mother Ailbhe?"

"Yes, she is."

"And you know not the power your blood holds?"

"My blood? Power? No, I—I'm just a nobody. Clumsy and forgetful."

Miri looked at me with dissatisfaction. "That's not true in the slightest, Torren, and you know it. Okay, some of it's true, but you're definitely not a nobody," she said.

"Hmmm. Yet, you come here looking for...What?" I, too, pondered the dragon's question at hand. What exactly were we looking for? I know my mother said I would know when I saw it, but I had no idea where to even start once we made it out of the tunnel.

"I don't know what it is, really. My mother just told me I would know when I see it."

"A cloak, boy. A cloak is what she sent you to find."

"We already found the cloak. Jordiah got his grimy hands on it."

"Jordiah?"

"Yes. He and his people raided our village, setting it ablaze searching for it."

"Werewolves. He must not get the second cloak. With one, he will be nearly unstoppable, but with both, even the dragons would run in fear."

"Well, that seems serious," Cormac said.

"How could the cloaks be that powerful? I don't understand it's just cloth, fabric woven together to keep warm," I said, flustered.

"Young Torren, make your way to the top of the if the mountain. If you and your friends live, all will be explained. Before you go, tell me, are you not a healer, a holder of light?" I stood for a second, letting the thought sink in.

"I guess I am."

"I know you are, it is in your blood. I can smell it," Zax stated. "I will meet you at the top. The path from here doesn't get any easier." As the dragon flew off, I realized just how massive and mystical the creature was.

"Woah," we gasped. The site was amazing. Not many people ever see a dragon from afar, and we were just speaking to one.

CHAPTER 7

Secrets Uncovered

En route to, hopefully, Eru Psyawla, Lorcan, and the others were making good time and nearing the end of the tunnel. The torches lit with blue and white flame all along the straight path.

"Is it me, or is this almost too easy?"

"Don't jinx it, Kyna," Aevin stated.

"All she's saying is that the path has been...uneventful," Lorcan remarked.

"There, just ahead! A ladder!" Lorcan ran to the ladder at the end of the tunnel. "Come on, guys!"

They approached the ladder and slowly started climbing. After a moment, they began to hear footsteps marching on the ground and the sound of cadences and singing from people outside. Lorcan, in front, stopped climbing and waited for the noise to clear. As the sound faded, he began climbing again for a brief time before coming to hatch in the side of the tree, just like the others. Lorcan slightly opened the hatch, peering through the crack. He saw no one around and figured now would be a good time to exit the secret tunnel from the tree.

"Who do you think you are, young man?" A voice called from below as Lorcan began climbing down.

"Uhhh...well...we mean no harm, sir. We've been attacked and came to warn the High Council." Lorcan said nervously.

"Attacked? VaHaile? Come down and explain what happened," the warrior commanded.

"Umm. O—Ok. Just a moment!" Lorcan stumbled on his words as he slowly climbed down the tree while the others followed.

"Tell me, what is your name?" The warrior asked politely. "Lorcan. And this is Aevin, Keela, and Kyna. And yes, VaHaile was attacked. Most of the people are hiding in tunnels underground. Some didn't make it. We came to warn Eru Psyawla." Lorcan talked fast.

"Okay. Okay. Calm down. Follow me, the castle is this way. And on the way, you can explain how you came from the inside of a tree." As the group followed the warrior through Eru Psyawla, Lorcan explained what had happened with the cloak and his hometown, as tears filled his eyes. He did not, however, explain the power that was discovered along their journey.

Once they arrived at the castle, the warrior led them to a hall, which was filled with beautiful, elegant drapes covering the walls. They were white and boarded with gold and green. And had the High Council symbol in the center, also green. It was different than the room and halls we had been in previously when we received our confinement. More calm and prestigious. Though the entire castle was beautiful, inside and out.

"The Council and the king will see you now." A different guard said, unamused. Lorcan, Keela, and the two others walked past the guard and through a doorway leading to a room with a polished wooden table and green curtains that covered the windows for privacy. There was a rug that lay on the floor, seemingly made of fur, perhaps from a bear, but it didn't look like fur they had seen before. It was a mix of grey, white, black, and brown. The way in which it was fitted together made it rather...magical.

"Have a seat, make yourselves at home. This is not court, there is no reason to be nervous," instructed the High Elf, Ralcord. They all then sat at the table, and the room filled with an awkward silence. They didn't know if they should speak first, or if they just let the High Elf go first. It didn't take long before other Council members entered the room. Zerrick, Malfae, Crisben, Zane, and the Queen, Valmera, all sat around the table looking at one another, and then looking at us.

"Good evening," Valmera greeted. "What brings you to the castle this time? And where are the rest of your friends?"

"Not to mention breaking their confinement," Zerrick added.

"High Council, King, and Queen, we did not break confinement, our village was attacked. It..." Lorcan paused. "It no longer stands. Most of the people are safe, some were unfortunate. We came here to send a warning."

"I am deeply sorry for the losses you have suffered. Do you know who is responsible for the attack?"

"Blasted werewolves. It's always the werewolves," Crisben muttered with frustration.

"Uh, yes, sir. Werewolves. Well, we believe it to be their kind."

"One moment," said the king, as all members turned toward him, and they began whispering.

Malfae then stood and walked briskly from the room and shouted "Rangers! On me!" as she passed through the door.

"Explain everything that happened, well, what you saw. And what the people looked like. A name, perhaps and where are your other friends?" Zerrick asked.

"The attackers were...hairy. And wore dark-colored tunics. I—I couldn't tell much more through the dark of the night and all the smoke," Keela explained with sadness in her voice.

"Jord—Jor..." Lorcan tried to remember the leader's name.

"Jordiah?" Ralcord asked with suspicion.

"Yes! That's it!" Lorcan exclaimed.

"Did he have a cloak?" Lorcan, Keela, and Kyna looked at each other with disappointment in their eyes.

"We had the cloak, but Jordiah took it from Torren. He and the others went on a separate path to the mountain. His mother sent him there, said that he must go and with haste."

"Yeah," Kyna added. "Said he will know what he is looking for when he sees it?"

Without hesitation, the king stood up and said, "Follow me. If the events in which I believe are about to take place, you are not safe. Especially if Jordiah has the cloak. We call it the Cloak of Ash. Another cloak, hopefully still hidden, we call the Cloak of Light," Ralcord explained.

"Explain, but you will have to wait for Torren to arrive to explain again. Or just write it down, perhaps?" Lorcan suggested.

"Guys. How much further does this thing go?" Cormac complained. We had been walking forever, it seemed, but we knew we had to reach the top. We didn't know if more dragons would be waiting for us once we got to the end, and if they were, would they eat us? We didn't know what to expect; we just wanted to be there already.

"Hopefully, not much further, Cormac," I muttered.

"I've said it before, I'll say it again, you guys need to exercise more. Strengthen those legs," Miri laughed.

"It's not just my legs that are tired. I'm hungry, my mind is a foggy mess, and I can barely keep my eyes open," I explained with a yawn.

"It has been an exciting few days, hasn't it? Tiring and... sad," Miri replied.

"Yes, and I feel like we won't rest for a while. I'm more worried about food and water. When was the last drink any of us had? Was that dragon back there real? Or were we hallucinating?"

"Yeah, Torren, we all hallucinated the exact same thing at the same time. Of course it was real!" Miri made sure I understood that what I was suggesting was ridiculous. In all honesty, though, we had traveled a fair distance and had had little to eat, and even less sleep. Not to mention all the excitement, and by excitement, I meant the terror and devastation of the last couple of days. We were all in shock. We can't forget about being confused. With all the lies and secrets our people were keeping behind closed lips, who knows what was right and wrong? What stories were we told as young elves that were, in fact, real events? These thoughts circled my head constantly as we ascended up the mountain path.

"When will you practice your new gift?" Cormac excitedly asked.

"I'm hoping the dragons will have some answers. If they don't eat us first," I replied.

"*Oh*, maybe they'll have food for us!" Cormac put his hand on his stomach and rubbed it at the thought of food in the near future. "Like some fresh makian soup, or mixberry bread with jam!"

"Cormac, I'm sure dragons don't cook their food before eating it," Miri informed.

We reached a section of the path where the roof was lower, the walls were closer together, and light was nonexistent; there were no lit torches now.

"Torren, see if you can use your power to light the tunnel," Miri instructed.

"I mean, I guess I can try, but what if it doesn't work and causes an explosion or something, and we all die?"

"I'm with Torren on this one," Cormac said.

"Come on, guys. Torren, you have to learn how this thing works sooner or later. And now we could really use some light."

"Okay. Stand back. Let's give it a go, I suppose." I held my hand out and tried to think about light coming from my hand while also thinking about not exploding us to bits. A small light flickered from my hand and quickly faded.

"Ahh, I can't do it. I don't understand. How can I walk up to a cursed unicorn and heal it with ease? And when I try to produce light from my hand, I can't." My mind was too cluttered and exhausted to concentrate enough.

"Just breathe, Torren. Clear your mind. You got this," Miri said while placing her hand on my shoulder.

"Okay. One more time." I tried again. Thus, the light was a little brighter and stayed a little longer, but I couldn't hold it.

"Uhhh," I grunted. "Almost."

"Here. Keep your hand out, close your eyes, and try again. Don't pay attention to anything else," Miri said, and as I closed my eyes and held my hand out, she reached in and kissed me, lips to lips. I was surprised, shocked, but calm. My mind was completely free in that moment. Suddenly, light gleamed from my hand, lighting the space around us. Miri and I continued to kiss when Cormac cleared his throat, alarming both of us.

"Oh. I just wanted to try to calm you down, is all," Miri said.

"O—oh. Okay," I replied, and cleared my throat. "The light's still there, so shall we?" I gestured, moving ahead with my hand. Miri smiled and walked past me, brushing up against my arm. It was nice. The kiss. It felt like something I had wanted for a long time but didn't know I wanted it. I couldn't help but wonder what her thoughts on the act were. We couldn't possibly think about relationships in such a pressing time as this. Did she like me in that way?

"So, are we going to talk about...you know...the kiss?" Cormac asked.

"Not now, Cormac. Maybe once this is over. For now, we need to find what my mother sent us for." I couldn't help but feel some sort of way about kissing Miri. It was pleasant and sensational. I noticed that after my comment, Miri had a certain look on her face that represented dissatisfaction. Was there something I was missing? The timing for such things was just not right. Once the kingdom was safe, or in utter destruction and all hope lost, maybe we could revisit the feelings we may or may not have and sort it out. For now, we would move ahead.

After much hiking through the wet and dark tunnel, the light in my palm had begun to fade. I was tired and getting weak. My arm felt as if I had been holding a sack of flour for hours. I honestly didn't think I would be able to hold it much longer.

"Guys, we need to rest," I sighed as I let the light fade out.

"Great, Torren. Now we can't see," Miri pointed out the obvious.

"Just a moment. My arm was dead, Mir. I couldn't hold it much longer. Using my power takes energy, and I'm exhausted," I complained.

"Well, we can't walk if we can't see."

"Cormac, I know. We could all use the rest, don't you think?"

"True. And I am hungry. Too bad we don't have much to eat."

Me, Cormac, and Miri search through our sacs and pockets for any leftover nuts or berries.

"Here." I held my palm open and let a dim light shine, just enough for us to see what snacks we might have. I was able to pull out four nuts, one berry, and a piece of string that surely couldn't be eaten. Miri pulls out two nuts, three berries, and a small piece of meat.

"Well, I suppose I forgot about this." Cormac pulled out a sack of meat strips from his pocket, which had ten thin pieces of meat.

"Cormac! You're a lifesaver!" Miri shouted in excitement.

"How do you forget about that?"

"Torren, it's been a very exciting, very scary couple of days. It just slipped my mind, I guess," Cormac explained. And it had been. Exciting and scary. With no telling how the rest of the adventure would go. And not just searching for a mysterious item my mother wanted us to find, but all of it. Jordiah, Eru Psyawla, our home. So much had already happened, and to think, just a couple of weeks ago, everything was calm and normal. Now, our home was destroyed, Lorcan, Keela, Kyna, and Aevin were who knows where, there were magic cloaks and secrets kept by the kingdom, and, apparently, my bloodline was powerful in some way. What else could happen?

We sat and ate our strips of meat, berries, and nuts in silence. Just trying to capture what might come next. After our snack, we dozed off for a moment, catching up on some well-needed sleep. It wasn't really intentional but definitely well-received. It wasn't a long nap. We awoke, startled by a loud and stern voice in our minds that said, "Keep moving!"

"Did you hear that as well?"

Miri and Cormac answered with "Yes."

"I guess we dozed for a moment."

"Yeah, but it was needed, I suppose," Miri yawned. "I guess we should get moving." I reached my hand out for the light to shine, and this time, it was effortless. White light gleamed from my palm, illuminating the tunnel around us. We treaded through the tunnel, and shortly after we started walking again, the ground began to level, the air was colder, and breathing was getting more difficult. We could hear snarls and low growls coming from ahead. A beam of light glistened as we turned the corner, indicating an opening. We used caution as we approached the lit opening in the tunnel, not knowing what would be waiting for us. Our eyes burned and squinted as they adjusted to the bright light shining through.

"Is it the end of the tunnel, or just another window?" Cormac whispered.

"I believe it is the end. Come on," I said, picking up pace toward the light. We stepped into the lit area, and we were filled with relief to realize we were standing outside on the mountain. It was the very tip-top, but we made it out of the darkened tunnel, finally. Once our eyes adjusted to the light from the sun, we saw patches of snow lying on the ground, and other areas were covered in greenery and flowers. Out on the horizon, the sunset laid an ethereal scene in the sky, a perfect end to a mournful and hectic day.

"The night will come soon. We should start looking for… whatever it is," I said just as a gust of wind blew past, and the sound of a snarl echoed above. We looked to the sky only to see Zax, the guardian dragon, floating above.

"I see you finally decided to ascend from the darkened tunnel, little ones," Zax said in our minds. "What you are looking for is a chest, hidden somewhere on this mountain. Possibly in a cave, or near the river's headwater. We were never told its location exactly, for reasons you will learn on the way. Your journey, however, starts there." Zax pointed to an opening in the mountain, a crack, right next to a thicket of bush covered in snow.

"Your power is just beginning, Torren. Do not be afraid to use it. You will find the answers to many of your questions once you find the chest and bring what it holds back to this point. I will be waiting. Oh, and do not fear the other dragons. They will not harm you unless you threaten them first," Zax explained. The way Zax spoke gave us a vibe of wisdom that comes from ancient beings. Which made sense; most dragons were ancient beings.

In Eru Psyawla, Lorcan and the others were led to a room below the main floor of the castle. It was darker but lit with the same blue and white flames that we had seen in the tunnels. The walls were lined with a dark marble stone, which had the High Council seal and the words *Instituendi ut Pugnare* engraved. The room gave off a dreary feeling, much different than the rest of the castle. There were tables with weapons neatly placed according to category.

"This is a training area, one of many below the castle. It is where the most sophisticated and elite battle preparation takes place; only a select few officials know of its whereabouts. Those words, there," Ralcord explained, pointing to the engravings on the wall, "mean train as you fight. We believe that if you train lazily and half-heartedly, then you will fight lazily and half-heartedly. A warrior, especially the elite, should fight with all their heart and mind until victory or death. The rooms here are designed to free our men of any distractions, except those brought on by the battlefield, and to train them to use their weapons and surroundings effectively." Ralcord walked over to the table that held the bows and quivers of arrows, picked up an arrow, looked at it intently, and sat it back down on the table.

"Why did you bring us down here, sir?" Kyna asked.

"You see, if there is about to be a war with the werewolves and Alpha Jordiah has one of the cloaks, we will need all the help we can get. You will all train down here in the war rooms with what little time we have. I will locate Malfae, member of the High Council as well as leader of the Ranger Brigade. She will be in charge of your training. Until then, find a weapon and familiarize yourselves with it. Become comfortable with it; it will be your best friend in the days to come."

"High Elf, sir," Lorcan cleared his throat, "I believe you were going to explain some things."

"Ah, yes. Well, long story short, there were sisters, two to be exact, with great power and even greater hearts. They stumbled upon an orb, one of six orbs known as the Orbs of Imperium. Both sisters wanted to hold the orb, and as fate would have it, they dropped the orb, fighting over it. Once the orb hit the ground, immense power surged through the earth below them, flowing into the fabric of their cloaks. Thus empowering the cloaks they wore and enhancing the powder they possessed. Now, not only did it heighten their powers range and strength, but the cloaks also then enabled them to learn new powers, much more powerful than recently thought. One sister betrayed her kind, falling in love and having a child with a werewolf. Her son..." Ralcord paused a moment and walked closer to us, standing just a few inches from Lorcan, "is Jordiah. So yes, Alpha Jordiah is a half-werewolf and half-elf who seems to have inherited his mother's powers. You can imagine the danger he poses to our race, especially while in possession of the Cloak of Ash." A heavy gasp echoed from the group.

"So, you knew this before, for who knows how long, and this is the first we are hearing about it? How many people know, or don't know? Torren was right, the kingdom is holding secrets. We deserve to know why, especially now," Kyna stated, placing her hands on hips.

"Ms. Kyna, I am the High Elf; you are lucky these are pressing times, or you would find yourself in more than just confinement."

An awkward silence and aggression filled the room for a moment. Crisben stepped forward, clearing the silence, "Ahem, I believe that is all for now. More answers will come later, once the time is right. Most importantly, Jordiah must not get ahold of the second cloak. You believe he is on his way here; Malfae is briefing the Rangers as we speak. They will gather the other warriors and prepare a stronghold outside of Eru Psyawla, hopefully slowing down the mangy wolves. That will be nearly impossible with the Cloak of Ash. Even more so if he finds the second cloak. And you said Torren and the rest of your friends are heading to the mountains, yes? At least he has a head start."

"What do you mean?" Aevin asked.

"The second cloak, the Cloak of Light, is in the mountains, well hidden. His mother was a healer. If he is in search of the cloak, he must have inherited the power. If not, the path to retrieve the cloak may kill him and your friends."

"That is all for now; we must prepare for what is to come. Familiarize and bond with your weapon," Ralcord said as he and the other Council members walked through the door and up to the main floor of the castle.

CHAPTER 8

The Cloak of Light

The passage through and around the mountain was proving to be far more challenging than any of us had imagined. We were sure that path wasn't taking us to the very top of the mountain but seemed to be leading near its peak. The wind was much colder, and the ground lay with snow and patches of ice, so it was hard to catch the correct footing for traction. Though the site was more dazzling than it was miserable, for now. We eventually came to a cliff, a ledge of sorts with a crack lying between where we stood and the side we needed to get to. It wasn't very wide, but there was no way we could walk around it, and it was just big enough that we definitely couldn't jump across. As we scanned the area intently, Miri noticed a slap of rock lying against the mountainside just off to our left. We tried and tried to move the slab of rock, but it was too heavy for the three of us to move by hand.

"Miri, you're going to have to move it with your power; it's the only way," I said, catching my breath from trying to move the rock.

"Just a moment. I'll try. I need to rest a quick sec first," she replied while sitting next to the slab. After a couple of minutes passed, "Okay. I'm ready. I'm not sure it'll work, though." Miri stood up and centered herself with the crack and just a few feet from the slap of rock, held her hand out, and closed her eyes. She opened them, and the rock began to rumble and shake. At that moment, Cormac and I moved back a few paces in fear the slab would fall on us. Miri inhaled deeply, then exhaled, and finally, the slab began to rise off the ground and float over the top of the crack. The rock slowly descended, laying across the crack, acting as a bridge. Miri then fell to her knees and let out a loud gasp. I ran over to her side, placing my arms around her.

"Are you okay? You did it. You did it, Miri! That was amazing."

"I'm fine, just...tired." Cormac helped me gather Miri to her feet and guide her across the bridge that she had constructed with her mind.

Once across, there was a cave surrounded by mountainside and nothing else. No other path, no trees or secret path. Just a dark, cold, wet cave. We grew frustrated with the idea of walking in a confined dark space again, but it seemed it was our only option. I stepped toward the opening of the mountain, and once I reached it, I was blown back a step and couldn't pass through the cave opening. Almost as if there were a force field keeping me out.

"What was that? Just walk in, Torren," Cormac instructed while walking up to the cave entrance and experiencing the same effect.

"I don't understand. It must be protected from trespassers," Cormac said.

"There must be a way in, though. Just hidden, maybe? Or a password of sorts?" I suggested. "We can't use Miri's gift to get past this one, that's for certain."

"Okay, there's got to be some kind of hint or...something telling us what to do. They couldn't possibly expect us to know how to get through the field protecting it. So, Torren, you take that wall, Cormac, that one, and I'll take this wall. Hopefully we find something soon. The sun is almost completely set, and it's getting far too cold." With Miri's command, we attentively scanned the walls of the mountain, hoping to find some way into the cave. Moving through snow and ice and pushing past bush after bush, we searched but to no avail. There was no switch, no hidden buttons, nothing that we could find that would let us through the cave entrance. We sat on a boulder sticking from the mountainside with a great sigh of disappointment.

"I don't know what else to do. We looked everywhere, pushed every rock, stone, and bush I could see, and still nothing," Cormac grunted. "We will freeze to death up here, and no one will know because the dragons will have our rotting corpses for a snack." With the temperature dropping and the breeze getting colder, I decided to use my gift as a warmer, if it would work. I held my hand in front of us, casting a light to heat the area around us, and I don't know exactly what happened, but I slipped on the boulder and grabbed the giant rock with my glowing hand. In that moment, there was a surge of energy that swept through to the cave entrance.

"What in blazes just happened?" Miri stood, shell-shocked.

"I—I don't know. I think...I think the entrance just opened," I replied, just as confused. We walked over to the cave and slowly entered into the cave, realizing the force field had disappeared.

The room was dark, so I used my palm to light the passage. In the illuminated cavern, we saw a glimpse of standing candles along the walls, leading further into the cave, but they were not lit. We had no way to light the wicks, and I knew I couldn't hold the luminance for long. *But maybe I can light the candles using my gift,* I thought. I reached my palm out and concentrated on spreading the light, but it only made the light in my palm brighter. Useful, but I would be exhausted by the time we got halfway through this darkened, wet cavern.

"Maybe walk up and try touching the wick?" Miri suggested.

"Wouldn't hurt, I suppose." I walked up to the closest candle and held the wick between the first finger and thumb. My hand gleamed with light, but the wick wouldn't flame. "Well, that's strike two."

"While we're inside, away from the elements, maybe just see what you can do? Practice a bit?" Cormac suggested.

"I'm afraid we don't have the time. This is my practice. This path, searching for, I assume, the second cloak, is my practice. You heard the dragon."

"I know, I just thought about maybe practicing here before we would give you time to figure out how to light the torches." Pacing the dimly lit cave, the light in my hand started to fade, and my mind was scrambling for ideas. *If we can't see where we are going, how are we going to find the chest?*

"I've got an idea, though, I'm not sure how safe it is," I said. "Stand back, next to the entrance." I walked a few paces away from the first torch and held out my hand and whispered, "Light the path before us," and a ball of light shot from my palm and flew down the tunnel, lighting each torch it passed with an orange and white flame.

"Okay. Now that's cool!" Cormac exclaimed.

"Indeed. It is. But it's odd. The flames are similar to the flames in the tunnels before, right? Just white and orange instead of white and blue."

"Torren, I'm sure the color doesn't mean much. Come on, let's get moving," Miri said, walking past me, eager to see the path ahead.

The flames lit all along the path, which was a much more zigzag-like line pattern. We came to a space that seemed just barely big enough to crawl through, but you could see light continue on the other side. On the wall next to the small hole was a painting of six circles, all in the shape of a circle. Surrounding them were six dragons, one of which depicted Zax.

"Six circles, surrounded by dragons," Miri said, bewildered.

"Yes, but why would they be on this wall? There are no words. It's just...circles and magical creatures. Surely a child didn't make their way down here and draw these on the rock," Cormac said.

"I don't know, Cormac, but they wouldn't let just anyone here. There are dragons all over; they'd notice a stranger up here, no matter how sly the person might be," I said. "I'll go first." I stepped to the opening and started crawling through headfirst. A few moments later, I was standing on the other side.

"Seems safe!" I shouted to the others, insinuating they could crawl through. The section of the cave in which I stood was shaped differently from the tunnel we just were. And just across from me stood an opening in the wall, leading to a different path. Stones of different shapes and sides lay spread out on the ground, almost in a specific pattern.

I was distracted by the room around me and didn't notice Miri emerging from the crawlspace. She bumped into me, knocking me back onto a stone. As my foot landed on the stone, it sunk to the ground, setting off a chain reaction of events that none of us saw coming.

"Well, that can't be good," I muttered.

"What?" Miri asked just as the wall surrounding us began to crumble and the ground shook, as a violent rage awakened underneath. "Cormac! Hurry!"

Cormac crawled as fast as he could through the small shaft while stone and dust filled the space around him, making it more difficult for him to move. Miri reached to help guide him out, but he was still too far away, so she climbed in. With one leg sticking out of the shaft and the rest of her body lying inside, she dug through debris and grabbed ahold of Cormac. The walls around us were still crumbling and falling; finally, Miri was able to pull Cormac through the crawl space. Suddenly, a giant boulder fell from the ceiling right over the top of them. Without thinking, I reached out my hand and shot a ball of light at the boulder, breaking it into pieces. Dust filled the air around Cormac and Miri as they staggered through rock and dodged falling debris. We managed to clear our way through to the door, which now was covered by falling rock and dust. We had to dig our way out or be buried alive. Digging and digging, we became exhausted, but adrenaline had kicked in because I was moving rock and boulder faster and faster. Still, more just kept piling on.

"Miri, can you move it?"

"I can try!" Miri held her hand and moved a pile of debris, but it wasn't enough.

"Okay. New plan. Miri, try holding the debris off of us and away from the door; I'll try blasting a hole through the rubble!" I loudly instructed.

Miri held off the falling rock just enough for me to concentrate, and I used my light to burn through the mess. We hastily staggered through the opening as it quickly closed from falling debris behind us.

"Let's never do that again, okay?" Miri sighed and fell to her knees, rolling on her back.

"Cormac, are you okay?" I asked as I laid him on the ground.

"I..." he muttered, followed by gibberish as he lost consciousness. I leaned over to check his breathing and the sound of his heart.

"He's alive but hurt badly, I'm afraid."

"A lot of rock crumbled on him, Torren. It doesn't surprise me. Oh, my!" Miri said, gazing at a gash on her right shoulder. A few more wounds sprinkled on her body, as they did mine, from the falling debris.

"Miri, come here," I said as I patted the ground next to me. Miri rolled onto her knees and crawled a short way, sitting next to me while Cormac lay on the other. I grabbed Miri's hand and placed the other on Cormac's chest. Within a few seconds, light gleamed from both hands and cast around both of them. A sigh of relief flowed from Miri as the light around her brightened, healing her wounds. The cuts on Cormac slowly faded, along with bruises on his head.

"Better?" I asked Miri as I took my hand off Cormac but kept hold of Miri's hand. Miri chuckled and smiled as she bowed her head. She seemed to be happy but nervous at the same time. I quickly looked down at our hands, still intertwined, and let go of my grip.

She clutched my hand tighter and pulled my hand closer to her with the other hand, looked me in the eyes, said, "I—I... Thank you, Torren," and laid her head on my shoulder. "We should rest for a while," Miri suggested.

"As good a time as any, I suppose," I replied, laying my head against hers as we drifted off into a short slumber.

We awoke not knowing how much time had passed. And we knew time couldn't be wasted, though the rest was well needed. Cormac sat up in a panicked startle, gasping and groaning, as if he had been underwater for several minutes too long. Miri and I awoke to the sound of Cormac's panic and quickly jumped to our feet.

"Oh, you're awake. How do you feel?"

"Better than being in that crawlspace. Does anyone know how long we've been down here?"

"No. Hopefully not too long. We need to get moving, and quickly. I'll see if there are torches we can use." I held my hand out, illuminating the darkness surrounding us. There were two torches, one to the left and one to the right. Both hanging on the wall next to another darkened path.

"Well, I guess my power can't reach through walls," I chuckled. I lit the torches with a beam of light, this time with much more ease. "I think I'm getting the hang of this."

Miri and Cormac followed me through the tunnel, hoping for no more surprises.

"Hey, guys, another painting, over there." Miri pointed to the wall on the right. The walls were covered with paintings that seemed to tell a story. The first picture we saw earlier with six circles surrounded by dragons we still couldn't make sense of.

"Looks like two people with a circle between them?" Miri questioned.

"I believe you're right. But what does it mean? The painting back there, this one. There is bound to be more, but there are no words explaining any of it," I said.

"It's telling a story, obviously," Cormac said confidently.

"Well, yeah, but of what?" I asked.

"Well, there are two people and a circle object in between them, right? And look, that person's cloak looks familiar, right?"

"Yeah, Cormac, it does. That's the cloak Jordiah has!" I exclaimed. The second person was wearing a white cloak.

"But what do the circles mean? We need to find more; there has to be more. These pictures are here for a reason."

"I bet you're right. But who would've drawn these?" I muttered.

"Hopefully, we find out along the way. Let's keep moving," Miri said.

The rest of our trip was much less exciting, and we did not dare complain after what we went through over the last few days. Although, we were beginning to feel hungry again. We came to a dead-end, dumbfounded. There was no ladder or rope to climb. No secret door or passage anywhere that we could find. I sat down, my back against the cold wall of the mountain.

"What now?" I muttered and started flickering light on and off in my palm. "It's weird, isn't it?"

"Huh? What do you mean, Torren?" Miri said as she sat down beside me.

"How you wake up one day, and everything is...normal. Go to sleep that night and wake up the next day, and everything changed."

"Oh. I mean. I wouldn't say weird, really. Just something that happens."

"Miri, it isn't something that just happens. There's more going on; I can feel it."

"And we will figure it out, especially with that light power you have now," Cormac said.

"I know, we have no choice. We have to figure it out, or...we all die," I said. "I mean, who knows may—"

"Hey, look at this. Torren, shine your light over here," Miri interrupted Cormac. I shined the light closer to the wall where Miri was pointing, and there were more paintings, only this time, they seemed to tell a story. One picture showed two people who looked as if they were fighting over one of the circle-shaped objects. Just to the right, the people were falling, and the object hit the ground. Little waves flowed from the object and connected to them.

"I don't understand these. Why couldn't they just write, with words, so we could read it? I mean, yeah, obviously, these people are falling, but what is the circle? And who are they?" I said with frustration.

As we scanned the wall, we found at least a dozen more paintings. They illustrated the person in the dark cloak falling in love with a werewolf, them getting banned from the kingdom, and next, they were at war...with Eru Psyawla. The other person from the first painting was fighting alongside Eru Psyawla. In one picture, the two cloaked people were battling each other, depicting the white cloak winning. There was one image that had all three of us bewildered. The dark-cloaked elf was standing next to a werewolf, holding a baby.

"Jordiah? Could that be Jordiah?" I asked.

"It does make sense. Jordiah does have the ears of an elf and invaded VaHaile with a pack of werewolves," Miri explained. "No wonder he's so full of anger and hate. He grew up without his parents and probably blames the kingdom for that. Secondly, he was probably told that the kingdom should belong to him."

"We still aren't sure the baby is him," I said.

"Come on. This must be the way out. We will worry about the paintings later. I'm hungry," Cormac said, standing next to a painting of arrows pointing up. The arrows were painted next to a group of six stones, in a single line, hanging on the wall. A closer look at the stones showed only one was a slightly different color.

"This one," I muttered. "How'd we miss this earlier?" I turned away from the stones, and as the light in my palm moved away from the stones, Miri noticed something.

"Hey. Move the light next to where the stones are sticking out." I turned my head back around but couldn't see the stones anymore. I moved the light closer to the wall, and the six stones slowly peered out of the wall.

"Look at that. You guys see that?" Miri and Cormac echoed, "Yes." I pushed the stone that was a different shade than the rest and stones just big enough for our feet slid out of the wall, treading up to the ceiling in a zigzag pattern. Almost perfect for climbing. At the last step, there was a hidden hatch connected to the ceiling. We opened the hatch and stepped out of the darkened cavern, not surprised to see it was nightfall.

We were standing next to a stream of water flowing next to the mountainside, which glistened in the moonlight. The way it reflected the stars certainly made the scene more magical. Powdered snow was sprinkled on the ground, gleaming from the sky above. Majestic. Almost like a scene from a dream. This now had become my favorite spot in all of Zynthia.

"A waterfall, and I'll bet there's a cave behind it." I almost didn't want to move. The thought of entering the blackness of another cold, wet cave didn't sit well with me. We walked the snow-covered mountaintop, hoping for a different trail or hint as to where we should go next. It was either the river or, unfortunately, to wander behind the waterfall and investigate. We saw no reason to go swimming down river at the moment, so the waterfall it was. The closer we got, the easier it was to see through the falling stream, and there was, in fact, an opening in the mountain.

"What is it with adventures and caves?" I complained.

"It's exciting," Miri replied to my rhetorical question. "Traveling into the unknown, discovering. The wonder and magic." Miri was thrilled, wandering around, exploring new things in dark holes; I, on the other hand, was well over it. I had the feeling Cormac was neutral on the matter because he was quiet. That, or he was just too tired to think.

There was no dry alternative to reach the backside of the waterfall. We stepped into the pooling, freezing water, thankfully not as deep as we imagined. The cave was smaller than the others we had dove into. We were soaked from plunging through the waterfall, so we huddled near the rock wall, and I used my light in a poor attempt to warm us. There were torches lit, circling the inside walls of the cave, so I was happy to know I didn't need to use my gift to light the cave; I was already feeling drained.

Across the dim lit cave, a dais with a chest hid in the shadows. The chest was made of green marble, or something resembling marble. I couldn't help but feel that I had seen a familiar looking container growing up, only the one here seemed a bit bigger. Where have I seen this craftsmanship before?

"Torren, are you okay?" Miri asked as I got lost traveling back to my childhood.

"Uhh...y—yeah. But I swear I've seen a chest or container like this somewhere. It's familiar. From when I was younger." Silence filled the room for a moment as I tried to remember. My mother was always crafting things, especially handmade gifts for friends and family. Finally, it came to me. My mother was outside sitting on her workbench, polishing a small box made of some sort of stone, similar in nature to the chest sitting on the dais.

"My mother," I muttered.

"Your mom, Torren? What about her?"

"Miri, I think my mother crafted this box. When I was little, she crafted a similar one for a family friend as a gift."

"Anyone could have made this."

"No, look closer. All the jewelry boxes and containers that my mother ever made, what do they have in common?" I pointed to the top corners of the chest.

"Torren, what in blazes would a chest your mom made be doing here?"

"Cormac, there's only one reasonable explanation. See, look here." I pointed to writing on the dais that said, "Only the Light can force the darkness out. Only light can open all doors. Blood of my blood, let your light shine."

"Your mom is, or was, a healer! But why all the secrets? I wouldn't expect your parents hiding this from you."

"I'm sure she has her reasons, Miri."

"Well, go ahead. Let's see what's inside, shall we?" I touched the lock on the chest and illuminated it with my palm. An amazing aura shimmered around the box as the lid sprang open. Inside lay a cloak with orange and green trim surrounding the edges. I reached in and grasped the cloak, still in awe that it belonged to my mother long ago.

"Well, put it on," Miri said. With my face in awe, I held up the cloak, admiring the beauty of its craft and the power I felt flowing through the fibers. I slid it on over my head and immediately felt immense energy flowing through my veins.

"Wow!" I exclaimed. "I—I can feel it." It was almost like being reborn. I felt more powerful, more alive than I have in my entire life. I felt the light shining through my body, like a million flames had been lit. "Now, let's go stop Jordiah."

We exited the cave, and I was immediately met by Zax.

"Aha. Well done, young Torren. Your mother and the kingdom will be proud. Tell me, did your question get answered along your journey?" Zax was excited to see me wearing the cloak.

"Yes. Though I may have more now. The paintings in the caves illustrate two people fighting over a circular object, that object falls to the ground, causing a wave of power? I think... That power gets transferred into the cloaks they were wearing."

"Correct, Torren. The fibers which the cloaks were made of are a rare material found around this mountain range. The Cloak you wear, along with Jordiah's cloak, are the only two of its kind. The circular objects you saw drawn on the walls were power orbs. The six Orbs of Imperium. The sisters were fighting over the orb. The force from hitting the ground caused the energy from the orb to flow through the ground. That energy was drawn to the material the cloaks were made from, thus absorbing into the fibers, making the wearer of the cloak powerful, or more powerful than they were previously. Your mother and her sister were the first owners of the cloaks."

I stood, shell-shocked that my mother had a sister, my aunt, and that she had never told me about it. She, nor my dad, had never told me any of this.

"Okay, what about the war? There were images illuminating a war. My aunt was fighting alongside the werewolves."

"Yes. You may or may not know that werewolves have fated mates. They do not choose their love. The love is chosen for them. Your mother's sister was fated to be with Alpha Conri. This was the first time different races would mate. The kingdom, ruled by Ralcord's father at the time, High Elf Relnor, did not take kindly to...races mating outside their own. For this reason, he gave both an option: either they separated and never spoke to one another again, or they would be punished. So, the mated pair told the kingdom they would never see each other again, only they lied. Alpha Conri and Elf healer Adora hid in Tenebrae. There, they gathered their pack and assembled an army to attack Eru Psyawla," Zax explained.

"We know that Jordiah is their son and that he wants to conquer Zynthia, or at least bring down Eru Psyawla," I said.

"And what about the other orbs?" Miri asked.

"The others are spread throughout different kingdoms in the world. The stones were made in the beginning, like the land and all the different animal breeds, etc. Long ago, well before my time, and yours, the orbs were all in one place, Vulzaria. The energy and power which flowed through that land were terribly potent."

"I've heard of that place. Don't they call it 'the land of the dead?'" I asked.

"Hmm. I suppose it's a fitting name," Zax grunted. "The energy from the orbs corrupted Vulzaria's people. They turned on one another, bloodthirsty and power-hungry. They craved the energy from the orbs. But their hearts were not in the right place. Had their hearts been pure, they could have thrived and changed the world for the better. It was the only time we interfered. We saw the influence and destruction that much power could cause, so we split them amongst the kingdoms, each with its own guardian."

"But why not destroy them if they cause all that chaos?" Miri asked.

"The energy inside the orbs must go somewhere. The orbs can be destroyed, sure, but the energy they possess cannot. As long as the energy stays in the orbs, at least we know where that power is. Except in your case, of course. There is more to explain, but now is not the time. You must go, save your kingdom and its people," Zax explained. We looked around for a moment, trying to figure out how to quickly and safely get down the mountain. Zax must have been reading our minds, or he knew by the expression on our faces as we scanned the area.

"There is a path down the mountain, just over that bank. It's fairly easy. Shouldn't take but a few moments to reach the bottom."

We went over the mountainside, and there was a clear-cut path traveling down the mountain. When we made it to the base, we were surprised when a family of unicorns emerged from the tree line. *"Neigh. Neigh. Chuff."*

"Hello, old friend, feeling better?" It was the once-cursed unicorn I had healed and her foals. "Mind giving me and my friends a lift?"

CHAPTER 9

Battle for Eru Psyawla

Disclaimer: Please be advised that the following chapter contains scenes of violence that involve descriptions of harm and death to both people and animals. Reader discretion is strongly advised.

Jordiah marched his pack just outside of Eru Psyawla. There, the pack was met by a blockade of soldiers. General Victor Bloomdale was standing front and center when invaders arrived. Jordiah, wearing the cloak of Ash, halted his pack of werewolves.

"A good day to die, don't you think?"

"You mean a good day for you? No, no. This will be your last unless you surrender to the kingdom. This is your only chance."

"Oh, I don't think we will be doing that. For what the kingdom did to my parents, to my pack. No. This is just the beginning." Jordiah raised his arms, emitting a mixture of red and purple around his arms, and the eyes of his pack began to glow. Though the moon was not full, with the Cloak of Ash, it did not matter. The pack began to transform into their more vicious form, howling and growling, scratching and clawing through their skin. Werewolves, when transforming, resemble a much larger wolf standing on its back legs, though they are much faster running on all fours. Their muscles grow larger and stronger, and they are much more agile and faster. The transformation looks very painful, if you ask me. And their senses are heightened to a whole new level. Also, they're harder to kill. Much, much harder to kill. Add in their healing factor, and they were nearly invincible. Jordiah laughed, mocking the shock of the soldiers' faces.

"Whoever said a wolf needs a full moon?"

"No matter what form you take, you'll still be six feet under by sunrise, Jordiah, son of the traitor, Adora."

"Ahaha," Jordiah gave an evil chuckle. "You'll die for those words, tree-thumper."

"*Ahhh!* Attack!" shouted the general. The Alpha quickly changed form, but because he was a mixed-breed, his transformation was a bit different. He didn't take the full form of a wolf. His fur didn't cover his whole body, and he didn't ever run on all fours. He did, however, gain the qualities of a werewolf, along with the power he possessed from his mother's side and the added power from the Cloak of Ash. Both sides fearlessly and ferociously engaged in the battle, the start of the second war between the two races.

The Ranger Brigade gained the upper hand just a few moments after the battle started. Jordiah had been battling General Bloomdale, who was exceptionally well with a blade of any type. He, however, had the ability to create a flame around his weapon. He could control that fire as if it were an extension of his own body, slashing and hurling the blaze at his enemy. And being around a silver blade caused fragments of silver to liquefy, making it possible to throw molten hot silver into the enemy's skin, delivering stunning blows and, in some cases, fatal ones. As the general and Jordiah were battling, Beta Sabastian attempted a sneak attack on General Bloomdale; however, that would be his last. Elf warriors are trained to keep notice of their surroundings at all times, using every sense at their disposal. General Bloomdale caught a glimpse of the Beta preparing to make his move, then, when Sabastian started his lunge toward him, the General quickly kicked Jordiah back, turned just slightly, and threw his shield with a velocity fast enough to decapitate Sabastian.

As Sabastian's lifeless, headless body reverted back to human form, Jordiah, in a rage, yelled, "*Ahhhh!*" and energy surged from his body, knocking back every elf within ten yards of him, some of which fell on the blades, killing them. And with one swift motion, Jordiah used his power to speed across to General Bloomdale as if he were a blur moving through the wind. No one saw exactly what happened, but seconds after the blur, Jordiah was standing next to the General with his arm through the General's chest. Werewolves throughout the battlefield cheered and howled. The elves were stunned, shocked that one of their leaders had died so soon in battle. And then the fighting continued, with more bloodshed from both sides, but the werewolves were inching closer and closer to the city gate.

Inside the gate, Lorcan and the others continued training as they heard battle cries echoing from outside the walls.

"Everyone, the battle is moving closer as we speak. Civilians are starting to join the fight. Against my judgment, the queen, with her fiery spirit, will soon be on the battlefield. I do not like it or agree. However, she is strong, and being on her bedside can be...deadly," High Elf Ralcord said as he entered the room. "I couldn't dare think what I'd do if something were to happen to her, so I shall join by her side in the fight. We live together; we may die together. I can think of no better way to go."

"What happens to the kingdom if you both die, sir?" Keela asked as she laid her sword on the table next to her.

"Our son, Renwick, will assume the throne. He is in a safe place. The enemy won't even smell him. And for his safety, no one will know where he is hidden."

After the brief conversation with the High Elf, the leader of the Ranger Brigade and member of the High Council, Malfae, burst through the room, returning from the battle. She had been checking on the progress of the attack in between training sessions.

"You must be ready; both sides are taking significant losses, ours more so. The Ranger Brigade is handling its own, but we can't hold off forever. The wolves are somehow more powerful than imagined. And the Alpha, Jordiah, is taking out groups of our men with a single blow."

"I—I...I don't think I can do it," Keela stuttered. "I'm scared."

"Young lady, I know that you have a kind, soft heart. But right now is not the time for kindness. It is the time for blood, and it's either theirs or ours that will spill on the earth. Use the love in your heart to protect those you care about. And you carry that love on the edge of this blade," Malfae said as she picked up Keela's sword.

Keela took the sword with a tear rolling down her cheek and said, "For my family, for my friends, and those who burned in our village."

"That's my girl." Malfae laid her hand on Keela's shoulder, turned, and walked out the door.

"So...do we go, too?"

Right after Kyna asked the question, Malfae popped her head through the door and said, "You're supposed to dramatically follow me onto the battlefield."

Jordiah and his pack had advanced closer to the gate. High Elf Ralcord and his wife, alongside a hundred or so guards, were waiting just inside the walls. All they could think about was the safety of the kingdom, its future. And that future was held with their son. Lorcan, Keela, Aevin, and Kyna arrived at the castle gates with Malfae.

"Your Highness, we are ready," Lorcan said.

"Once we move beyond this gate, we may never return. Valmera, I love you."

"I love you, too, Ralcord."

They followed the king to the right of the gate and stopped next to a flower garden connected to the wall.

"Here, a secret passage leading out of the kingdom. You cannot enter through this way. For that, you must use the main gate doors. This will allow us to arrive on the battlefield without leaving the entrance vulnerable. These flowers here mask the scent from the wolves. They could be on the other side of this wall and never know we were here. Can any of you tell me when your friend Torren should arrive?" My friends shook their heads "no" in response. "Well, hopefully, he hurries. We will need him to stop Jordiah."

"We are talking about the same Torren, right?" Kyna asked.

"Yes, Torren Luxmin, son of Ailbhe. He is more important than you know. He is a Healer. And once he has the Cloak of Light, only he can stop this madness." Ralcord lifted a yellow flower from the garden and the wall slid open, creating a small door. Together, they marched onto the battlefield, not knowing who would live and who would perish. Frozen for a moment, taking in all the destruction and bloodshed around them, Keela fell to her knees in silence and closed her eyes. A moment later, she stood with her eyes focused and blade drawn.

"Let's drive these mangy dogs back to where they came from."

The group of friends ran into battle with their weapons drawn, their hearts set on fire, and their eyes focused. They knew it wouldn't be easy; they knew they may not make it out alive. But they knew if they didn't at least try, Jordiah and his pack of wolves would devour them anyway.

The group of friends tried to stay together; that way, they could watch each other's back. But after a while of fighting the werewolves, the group slowly began dispersing. Lorcan eventually found a good vantage point to pick the wolves off with his bow and silver-tipped arrows. One by one, arrow by arrow, the wolves quickly found themselves diminishing in number. Keela and Kyna found their way back to each other.

"What happened to your leg? Are you okay?" Keela saw a gash on Kyna's leg.

"I'm fine. It'll take more than a scratch on the leg to put me down," Keela replied while thrusting her sword through an adversary. Aevin had fallen on the ground just a few feet away from the twins, and just as one of the wolves started to pounce on top of him, an arrow whizzed by his head and landed in the wolf's chest.

Aevin gasped and yelled, "Thank you, Lorcan!" with a thumbs up. He quickly stood to his feet and began fighting again with his silver spear.

The Ranger Brigade had managed to push back the enemy while Jordiah took a quick breather. The power he was using was draining his energy. Yes, the cloak allowed him to use his power longer; still, he had been fighting since the start. Everyone was getting tired and hungry. The soldiers from the kingdom had a system in place to help with exhaustion. A group of soldiers would fight until they began feeling too winded; at that point, a rotation of fresh soldiers would take their place. And the cycle would repeat. Jordiah caught on, eventually, and started targeting the replacement soldiers. This was a great loss for the kingdom. Elves had great stamina, but a werewolf's stamina was far greater. Especially when that werewolf is enhanced with magic.

The sun had started to rise as the battle continued, and the werewolves had managed to push right next to the gate. A couple of the werewolves had managed to jump over the gate, attacking anyone on the other side. Lorcan picked off a couple attempting the feat, which Jordiah found very frustrating. He attempted to make his way closer to Lorcan but was met by a group of Rangers, Malfae, Haldor, Breeck, and Balten.

"You really think you can stop me, stop us? Fools! Imbeciles! I grow tired of this...this game," Jordiah shouted and grunted as he lifted himself into the air and hovered above the Rangers.

"This is it. Stay right there, you mutt," Lorcan muttered as he released an arrow heading straight for Jordiah's head. Just before the arrow landed, Bella, Jordiah's fate mate, jumped in the air, allowing the arrow to pierce her side, saving her love.

"No!" Jordiah sighed. He floated down to his mate's side, holding her up. "My love, Bella. Can you hear me?"

"I—I'm here," Bella muttered. Jordiah grabbed the arrow and plucked it from her side.

"You'll be okay, dear. You'll be okay."

Jordiah used his magic to try and heal her. He was able to close the wound somewhat, but the silver fragments inside the wound wouldn't allow it to heal completely. The silver embedded inside her flesh and blood had made it impossible for her to continue the fight.

"Gram! Felix! Over here, now!" He called the closest members of his pack. Soldiers and werewolves were fighting all around them as Jordiah focused on his mate.

"Take her back, do what you can. There is a bag with supplies; you know where it is. Hurry," Jordiah instructed. "I love you, my dear. That archer will pay dearly." Jordiah stood on his feet, filled with anger and a new level of hate; he cried out the loudest battle cry anyone had ever heard. A wave pulsed through the air, and his pack grew a foot taller; their muscles were stronger, and they were much, much more terrifyingly ruthless. It was as if Jordiah had transferred his anger and hate into the wolves.

With their new growth in power, the wolves finally broke through the walls surrounding the kingdom. The people of Eru Psyawla were doing all they could to even scratch the wolves invading their home. Lorcan and the others retreated back after fighting a crowd of wolves, which were eventually, and thankfully, distracted by the Ranger Brigade. They managed to find a haven in a tower separated from the castle. They could hear the screams and growls echoing below them. Lorcan wanted to use his last few arrows to slow down the raid, but Aevin stopped him.

"Save them, we may need them if the pack makes their way up here. Plus, it would give away our position." The group was scathed, nearly broken-willed, and exhausted.

"Where the dragon's fire is Torren?" Kyna grunted.

"He will be here as soon as he can. Just have faith," her sister replied.

"You did good out there, sis."

"You, too. We all did."

"Wouldn't happen to have any food on you, anyone?" Aevin asked, holding his stomach.

"Unfortunately, no. Hey. Look out there, Lorcan, see if you can lay eyes on the king and queen," Kyna said.

Lorcan peered out of the tower window, eyeing the devastating bloodshed throughout the kingdom. The pack hadn't reached the castle yet; the Rangers and some civilians were holding them off. A wolf was about two seconds away from chopping a civilian's head when a Ranger quickly fired spikes of ice from his hand, lodging them in the back of the beast's throat.

"I don't see any sign of them. But the Rangers seem to be holding their own."

"We need to make sure they are okay," Keela stated while crossing her arms.

It was about mid-morning; the group had decided to leave the tower and make their way to find the High Elf and the queen. Lorcan peeked through the door to check the surrounding area for any sign of danger. Seeing no threat, he motioned to his friends it was safe to advance. They walked around buildings and lifeless bodies. Approaching a broken-down shop, they spotted Malfae lying on the ground. She was wounded, fatally if not treated soon. Malfae grunted and moaned as Keela lay beside her.

"Shh. Shh. We're here, you'll be okay. You'll be okay."

"Keela, they must not reach the castle."

"They're close, but your men are strong, holding them back with the help of other soldiers and civilians. We're making our way there now."

Lorcan and Aevin grabbed Malfae and moved her to a more secure and safe location not far from where they were.

"Leave me with her. Someone has to stay with her."

"Sister, are you out of your mind? You're coming with us." Kyna pulled her sister to the side, and they began arguing.

"We can't just leave her here to die. She's the leader of the Ranger Brigade, for crying out loud. She's done more in one week than we ever will. Not to mention, she trained us in the short time we had before joining the fight. Without her help, we wouldn't have survived."

"I will not let you stay with her and die. If you're going to die, it'll be by my side."

"Kyna. I'll be fine. We will be fine. I'm staying." Keela walked back to Malfae and sat by her side, covering her with a sheet she picked up from the ground. The friends hugged and said their goodbyes. Kyna grasped her sister and squeezed her sister tighter than she ever had, letting the moment hang for a moment.

"Come on, we should get going," Lorcan said.

Following the wall surrounding the village seemed to be the best route. Once they reached the wall surrounding the castle, they could follow an alleyway that went right up to the gate on the backside. The path was lined with trees of different breeds and sizes but made great cover for us approaching the castle. It was actually a terrible design. It could allow a stranger safe passage to and over the wall, if they were a good climber. And that's exactly what they planned to do. They were hopeful the smell of the sap from the trees would mask their scent. Aevin spotted a group of people hanging around a garden, acting sort of weird. They didn't look like locals, and they were naked. They pulled clothes from a sack and put them on. One of the men started sniffing the air.

Aevin got the others' attention as the person was starting to sniff in their direction. Then he got his friends' attention and said, "Hey, I got something. Over here," and pointed right at Aevin and the group, hidden behind a thicket of bushes.

"Go. Go, go, go," Aevin whispered, speaking fast. "Run!"

On the quiet command from Aevin, the group ran as fast as they could down the street and turned into an alley with bins, benches, and tables, along with some other miscellaneous items. Hiding behind anything they could find, Lorcan caught a glimpse of something that resembled a hand.

"Ahh, leave them be, for now. Whoever it was has nowhere to go. We'll snack on them later." The sound of footsteps faded as their hearts raced. Lorcan waited a brief moment to make sure the wolves actually retreated, then got up and walked toward the hand. He got closer and saw more of the face.

"Mr. Flantly?" He bent down for a closer look. "Guys, look. It's Mr. Flantly." He had been mauled by one of the wolves, or multiple, but you could still recognize him. There was no sign of his wife or her demise, but judging by the look of her husband, it was hard to believe she made it out alive.

"Listen, do you hear that?" Kyna asked, turning her head sideways to get a better listen. There were screeches, like metal clanging on metal, just on the other side of the alley. Kyna moved a table, very quietly, and climbed on tip to peek over the stone wall of the alley. A group of soldiers were battling three werewolves, while another group of werewolves changed form and took off in the direction of the castles.

"Three wolves, five soldiers. I don't see Jordiah. Three wolves took off that way, but in human form."

"How do you know they're wolves?" asked Aevin.

"Well, they were stark naked running toward the castle, so you tell me," Kyna replied with a look of disgust.

"We need to get to the castle. We know it's going to be dangerous, but we can't just stay here," Lorcan said.

"What about Torren?"

"He will know what to do when he gets here, Aevin. We need to see if the High Elf is alive, as well as his son."

"We don't know where they have him hidden. No one does, except the guards who are with him," Kyna said.

"We just have to pray they're safe. Come on. We need to go."

The friends exited the alley, heading towards the castle in the middle of the village. Avoiding the pack was nearly impossible as they were scattered around like beads thrown on the floor, creating havoc and destroying buildings, especially those with the High Elf's seal. The townsfolk, with aid from soldiers, were doing their best to defend their homeland. Many would meet a terrible end, unfortunately. Both sides had experienced heavy loss, but the pack surely had the upper hand with Jordiah's newfound power from the Cloak of Ash and marching closer to the castle.

It had just started to rain as the group arrived at a burnt-down market right outside the castle wall. The rain would mask their scent for the time being, allowing them to make it over the wall. Lorcan noticed a tall building just off to the right, but further from the direction they needed to go. He figured it would provide a good vantage point to look over the wall to see if there were any werewolves on the other side. With that idea, he quickly scanned the area for any adversaries and sprinted to the tower. He safely made it to the top and peered through the window. The castle yard was scattered with soldiers from Eru Psyawla, ready to defend the castle. He was able to spot the king and queen walking into the castle, though the king seemed to be injured as he was being aided by two guards. Off to the south, near the main entrance to the village, he saw the battle amongst the Rangers and a majority of the pack, including Jordiah.

"Better now or never, I suppose," Lorcan muttered." He raced down the steps and exited, running towards his friends. "It's safe. We can enter the castle gate. We should be able to move through the front. There are guards there. They'll let us in." He continued to explain what he saw from the tower. They moved to the gate, keeping their wits, and knocked, gently, so as not to draw attention from the wolves battling just over a couple of streets.

A guard stood at the gate and said, "If this is a wolf, we are manned and ready to defend the castle. If this is an ally, what is the password?"

"Password? No one mentioned a password to us. There are wolves just a couple of streets down. If you do not let us in, we are as good as dead!" Kyna said.

"The password, or I cannot let you in. I am sorry."

"Ughh," Kyna grunted with frustration.

"Uh…uh…" Lorcan thought for a second. "Uhh…Train as you fight."

"I'll take it. But if you even look like a threat, I'll cut your head off," the guard replied. As they entered through the gate, the cries of battle behind them quickly faded. Soon after, the air filled with an overwhelming silence, sparking a sense of unease amongst the people inside the walls. Was the battle over already? There were no howls echoing in the wind nor a cheer yelled. Finally, through the pouring rain emerged Rangers and soldiers, some carrying bodies of fallen comrades or injured folk, some with their heads held high and weapons in their hands.

"They fled. Jordiah got word of Luna Bella's wounding and retreated back to his village. He swore he'd return." Ranger Dax informed, carrying Malfae. Guards rushed down to take her on a stretcher, but Dax refused. He felt it was his place to carry his leader home. She was still breathing, but barely. Keela was in the group approaching the castle. Soldiers found her and Malfae walking back to the castle after the retreat.

"Did Jordiah's mate die?" High Elf Ralcord asked with worry in his voice.

"No, but by the sound of it, it's serious. The silver is in her bloodstream, making it difficult for her wounds to heal. Lorcan landed a pretty good shot. He's…pretty good with a bow," Dax said.

"Thank you," Lorcan said.

"Well, we might as well rest up and fill up while we can. If she dies, Jordiah will use all of his power to destroy everything in his path. He's already bent on revenge; if she dies, all that will remain in his heart is hate. As of now, we still have the advantage. And where is Torren?"

"High Elf, Ralcord, we thought he would be here by now. He, Miri, and Cormac surely wouldn't have encountered too much trouble with his newfound gift," Aevin said.

"His gift is greatly needed and will be in the days to come. Healers are very rare. But more powerful than they know. The light inside them can set the world on fire, or light the path for new beginnings, simply put. Or a combination of both, if they prefer. Come, let's go inside. It's been a long, long day," the High Elf said.

The battle didn't last long, but with devastating blows on both sides, neither would complain about a brief intermission. The High Council knew Jordiah and his pack would invade again, and soon. Rest and replenishment were top priorities. The group of friends was escorted to quarters, which housed beds, a couple of tables, two latrines, and a couple of miscellaneous items for grooming and recuperating. On the coffee table centered in the room lay a basket of fruit, nuts, sweet bread, assorted pastries, and a pitcher of coffee. Without hesitation, they gobbled down the tray of food and sipped on a delicious cup of the finest coffee they had ever tasted. After the cup of coffee, they were just about to fall asleep when suddenly the sound of neighs echoed just outside the castle. Kyna pulled back the curtain and looked out the window.

"Oh, now that's surprising and sort of wicked."

"What is it?" Keela and the others rushed over to Kyna's side.

"Torren?" Aevin said, dumbfounded.

Jordiah and his pack had retreated just outside the burned village of VaHaile. His mate, Bella, lay on a bed made from hay and grass, covered with a blanket found in one of the scorched houses in the village. Her body, littered with silver, was refusing to heal, and Jordiah's heart grew colder and colder, not knowing that was even possible. The rage built inside him as he watched, helpless, as his wife lay dying.

"They will pay. I will burn them to the ground and scatter their ashes across the land as a reminder never to oppose me. If she dies, the world dies with her," Jordiah growled.

Bella moaned and whispered to her love, "Reclaim our land, our home," and then lost consciousness. Jordiah panicked, shouting her name and rubbing her face.

"Please wake up, my dear," he whispered. Jordiah could feel his power weakening as his mate's health deteriorated. Which is the main reason he commanded the pack to retreat from Eru Psyawla. He needed his mate, not only for companionship, but also to keep at full strength. There would be a full moon tonight, which would aid in invading the castle once more, but Jordiah would have to attack as ferociously and swiftly as possible in order to claim victory. He had a plan. He called the new Beta, Xavier, and Gamma Theo, to assemble a meeting.

"There will be a full moon tonight. My power weakens every second my love lay on that bed of straw, dying. I will not be able to help you all hold form when we go to battle next. But tonight, we must strike hard and fast and surprise the enemy. Theo, you will lead troops around the back side, I will approach from the front, and Xavier will lead from the east. We will split the pack, but not evenly. "Theo added. "The majority can attack from the front, in hopes the elves won't see the attack from behind, or from the east. It'll be dark, so we have an advantage in the shadows."

Jordiah, Xavier, and Theo went to Bella's bedside to examine her condition and say goodbye, but Bella had other plans. With her health so fragile, transforming, even with Jordiah's magic and the full moon's help, she would not be able to change. Still, she insisted that she be carried to battle as she stood on her feet.

"Love, Jordiah, this will be a victory I long to see with my own eyes and will earn with my hands. I am the mother wolf, let me fulfill those duties and aid my pack, while I still can." Jordiah stared into her eyes and nodded, accepting his mate's request.

CHAPTER 10

Welcome Back with a Surprise

"So, it seems you had quite the adventure," Lorcan said as he walked me, Miri, and Cormac to the room they were staying in.

"Yeah, it was...exciting, I suppose. You should've seen Zax, though. Magnificent. Wise. You guys would have loved it. And you, Lorcan, killed the Luna?"

"I wouldn't say I killed her, Torren. She was hurt pretty badly, though. It just frustrates me. I could have ended the battle before they made it inside the wall, but she had to jump in front of the arrow."

"Well, one thing is for sure: hurting her is going to hurt Jordiah, which hurts the entire pack," I replied.

"You did good, all of you," stated the High Elf as he approached. "But we must be prepared for another attack. They're wounded, like we are, but not dead. They will return. And tonight is a full moon; I assume they will use that to their advantage. Found your mother's old cloak I see, Torren."

"Yes, sir. And we learned a lot from Zax, as well. My mother left paintings along the path, illustrating her and her sister's journey, finding one of the Orbs of Imperium, the war," I said. "Though, I don't understand one thing."

"What would that be?" Ralcord asked.

"Well, why are they secret, and what happened to my mother's power?" I asked.

"You know about the orbs, and that each one is protected in a different kingdom. Each orb contains power similar to the power the cloaks hold. It is believed that the orbs in one area would...overload and cause mass destruction. Some believe that tale is nonsense and having the orbs in one kingdom would empower that kingdom beyond anything we've ever imagined. As for the cloaks, they could not be destroyed because the power they possess is too great. So, hiding the cloaks seemed to be the best option, as to not tempt anyone curious enough to try them on."

"Okay. So, the kingdom kept it secret so that younger generations wouldn't search for that kind of power?" Miri asked.

"More or less...yes, Ms. Masel," Ralcord replied and continued. "Your mother had to use an extreme amount of power to stop her sister. The power was so great it killed the darkness in Adora. Unfortunately, the darkness was all she had left, so when the darkness inside Adora died, so did she. Your mother was so sorrowed and unable to forgive herself that her light faded. She vowed to never regain her power after that, and no one questioned that decision."

As we continued our walk, I heard moans echoing down the hall. The closer we got, the more I could hear the intensity of the sound. Keela explained what had happened as we stood in the doorway of the room in which Malfae lay, in pain and dying. A couple of guards stood at her bedside, and one said, "Mind your business. Let her rest."

"May I?" I walked into the room and stood inches away from Ranger General, waiting for a response. The guard looked at Malfae then quickly turned to his partner, and they simultaneously nodded and stepped aside.

I kneeled down by Malfae, placed my hand on hers, and whispered, "Thank you for helping my friends and for your service. This may be uncomfortable at first, but you'll thank me in a moment." I closed my eyes, and I could feel the pain she was in, the suffering she had endured. She was near death. My hand illuminated around hers, and she began to moan and groan louder, more intensely.

The guards then stepped toward me, ready to draw their weapons and dispose of me, but Miri halted them, saying, "Just a moment, trust him." The light gleamed around her hand and quickly glistened her entire body.

The light grew brighter, and she let out a very loud *"Ahhhhh!"* and went silent. The glow dimmed as I released my hand, and she sprung her eyes open wide with a deep inhalation of oxygen. She frantically felt her body and sat up, looked at me, said, "Torren!" and wrapped her arms around my neck, squeezing with enthusiasm, repeating, "Thank you!" as we swayed slightly left to right.

"I'll never get used to that," Aevin said.

"I can't believe it. Well, I can," Malfae said and then cleared her throat. "Excuse my...over enthusiasm. I shouldn't act so...

childish. But I do thank you, Torren. Now I can continue the fight."

"You're most welcome. How do you know my name?" I asked.

"You do have your mother's eyes, and you're wearing her cloak," Malfae replied. "Now, if you'll excuse me, I have a battle to win." Malfae stood up and stormed toward the door.

"They retreated, remember?" A guard told her.

"Oh. Yes. That's right. Well, they will be back. So, I guess I'll gather the Ranger Brigade and plan for the next attack."

"If you don't mind, after we get settled, eat, and rest a bit, I'd like to join in," Malfae agreed to my request, and continued to the Rangers' quarters.

Back in the room, I was munching on some sweet bread with berry jam, looking out of the window. *How I wish I was up in my tree right now.* I looked down near the stables and saw the unicorns that gave us a lift to the village. But it is great to have experienced the events leading to now. I stared at the unicorn I rode, the one that was cursed.

"Cloud. Thorn...Uni?" I muttered. "No. Surely not those names."

As I tried to think of a name, I flickered light with my hand like a tick. I wasn't really aware I was doing it. Only when it shined bright enough, I caught a glimpse out of the corner of my eye. The sunlight bouncing off her horn and fur and gleamed with a beautiful aurora through the air around her. Illuminating bright colors from her horn. Bright...beautiful power. *It's amazing, the luminance I create. The light hitting your horn, your fur. It's...*

"Aurora!" I shouted. Everyone in the room stared at me as if I were crazy. The unicorn looked up at me as she heard me shout her newfound name.

"What, Torren?" Miri asked, dumbfounded.

"Oh. Uh...I was just thinking of a name for the unicorn. Aurora."

"I like it," Miri said. "It's fitting." She walked over and looked down at the unicorn, putting her arm around mine.

"So, we should probably get some rest before the second battle starts."

"Yeah. For sure," I stuttered. Remembering the kiss back in the cave. Miri laid her head on my shoulder and sighed.

"It's a beautiful day, don't you think?" I nodded in agreement.

"It sure is, Mir. I just worry about tonight. We are all exhausted. Even if Jordiah isn't at full strength, he will be hard to stop. He's so full of hate and revenge, even more so that his mate has been wounded." I turned away from the window and faced my friends. "Okay. Let's rest up. It'll be a long night."

Later that evening, I awoke to the sound of Aurora neighing and chuffing and walked over to the window to check on her and the foals. They were restless, tired of being tied to a post. I walked down to the stable and stood in front of Aurora, petting her muzzle. I noticed they had no food to eat, or water.

"I'm a terrible unicorn owner, aren't I?" I pressed my head against her. I could feel how anxious she and the young ones were. Unsettled by guards and parents yelling at the children to get to the safe place before the sun went down, the tension and anticipation hung in the air like the nauseating smell from rotting briskberries.

"Here. This should do the trick. Eat up." I gave the unicorns some food and water, and as they were eating, a child ran up to me, her parents chasing her.

"Hello, I'm Beatrix. That's my mom, Valerie, and dad, Marcus. What's your name?"

I smiled softly, bent down to her level, and said, "My name is Torren. Me and my friends are from VaHaile. We are here to help defend against the werewolves."

"*Oh*. Uh…can I pet your horsey?" Beatrix asked with a smile from ear to ear. I looked at Aurora and back to her parents and nodded. I lifted Beatrix up after getting approval from her parents and guided her hand to Aurora's side. Her eyes lit up like stars across the night sky as her hand gently grazed through Aurora's fur side to side, up and down. Aurora's tail began to swing free and relaxed, and she was snorting and blowing sounds of acceptance of Beatrix's loving touch.

"Thank you, sir. It's been a very emotional day for all of us. She's so happy now," Valerie said.

The little girl turned and gave me the biggest leg hug ever and repeatedly said, "Thank you!" The family was finally able to persuade their daughter into the safe shelter after a few moments chatting, and a few more hugs from Beatrix. I made sure the unicorns had enough to eat and drink, then untied them and went for a stroll through the village.

We passed groups of people standing next to piles of debris and ash. Some were crying, others were picking up pieces and beginning to rebuild their establishments. Smoke still climbed through the air in most places, though it was dying out a little. Me, Cormac, and Miri had missed the first battle searching for the cloak. We were fortunate, or maybe unfortunate.

If we had been here, we could have aided in the defense. I could have used my power, cloak or no cloak, and possibly healed some warriors or blinded the wolves as they attacked. I suppose there is no way of telling what would've happened, or what will happen going forward.

Aurora's foals were following close. I didn't feel right leaving them behind, tied to that post by the stables, so I let them come along. They seemed fairly excited about the adventure, as did I.

As we approached the main gate, I expected the guards to open the doors, allowing us to flow right through. Instead, both of the guards blocked the doors as we got closer, yelling, "Halt!"

"What seems to be the problem?" I asked.

"Where are you headed?"

"Just going for a little walk, run, or whatever you'd call it. They were feeling restless and thought they'd want to roam for a bit," I replied.

"It may not be the best idea to roam outside of the gate with those mangy beings somewhere out there."

"Don't worry," I said, with a moment of silence filling the air. "I plan to go towards the mountain. The werewolves will be in the opposite direction. Besides, they are healing and waiting for the full moon tonight. We will be fine."

"It's your funeral, young man." The guards stepped aside and opened the gate, allowing me to pass.

We entered the forest and stopped at a meadow not too far from the village. It was glazed with beautiful blue and pink flowers sprinkled on the ground. They danced in the wind so freely and calmly; it was as though the meadow itself was singing a song. A beautiful day, indeed. I dismounted Aurora, and we began walking among the meadow. The young foals decided to begin playing and running around each other with much excitement. They were free. They were happy. With the foals distracted and no present danger lingering, I turned toward Aurora and laid my hand on her side.

"I am not sure that I'll be able to protect you and your foals from Jordiah. I'll do all I can to keep you from being cursed by him, but if it does happen and he manages to curse you or the young ones, I beg that you remember your friends." After I spoke, a thought came to me. If Jordiah could curse unicorns, maybe I could give them a power of sorts, somehow.

I climbed on Aurora, took a deep breath, and whispered, "Okay. I'm going to try something. Just go with it." I closed my eyes and placed both hands on her sides. After a moment, she began to chuff and snort and quickly followed with gentle bucking. Once she calmed down, I opened my eyes, and my heart was filled with joy. Her horn was glistening with a mixture of color, vibrant and bold. Her eyes shined as bright as the stars as she gazed into the meadow. She looked determined and ready for anything.

"Okay, girl, let's see what you can do." Her foals looked intently as we raced through the meadow. Perhaps dumbfounded at their mother's glowing form. The light shining from her horn streamed through the air as we galloped through the flowers, but nothing more was happening. It definitely wasn't as spectacular as I expected. The light would be good to get us spotted by the opposing side, but that is something we wouldn't want. Slightly frustrated with the lack of power, I gathered the unicorns and headed to the castle as the sun was beginning to set. Though, I was impressed with the way her horn and eyes illuminated.

We approached the castle while the sun was still hanging high but starting to descend. The warriors of Eru Psyawla were preparing to defend the village for a second battle. One we knew would soon transpire and bring with it the fury of Jordiah and his pack. I tied the unicorns next to the stable, near hay bales, and a trough for water so they could replenish with rest and energy before the next attack. The atmosphere around the castle was becoming more tense as the night fell upon the kingdom. Sorrow still filled the halls of missing loved ones and burned-down homes. I wondered how the people of VaHaile were managing in the dark tunnels. *Did they have enough food? Have they been caught?* All sorts of questions circled my mind. I couldn't risk going down there now. They would have to hold out a little longer, after the next battle. Making my way to the quarters where me and my friends were staying, I spotted Malfae waiting at the door.

"And where have you been all day?" she grunted with an unpleasant look on her face. I cleared my throat and replied, "I was just outside the village, walking with the unicorns. They had been tied down all day, so I figured they would want to stretch their legs."

"Mmhmm. You could have been attacked and killed. Did you think about that?" Malfae continued to berate me. "What would we have done then? No one else here can compete with Jordiah's power. No one else has the ability to stop this war."

"I—I'm sorry. I just wanted t—"

"Wanted to what, Torren? Believe the world is safe? Believe that because you're a healer, you can't die? Well, you can."

As I held my mouth open, trying to get a word in, she walked past me, grazing my shoulder. I didn't understand what I did wrong. I mean, yes, it might have been a little dangerous to go outside the gate, but Jordiah surely wouldn't attack in broad daylight with limited power. Even with my newfound power, I couldn't seem to do anything right.

Miri, Lorcan, and Kyna had woken just before I walked through the door. There was a fresh pot of coffee steaming on the table. They must have anticipated the group waking up and delivered some coffee and snacks, which is much appreciated and accepted. I was starving and incredibly grateful for the hospitality of the castle servants.

"Everybody! Come on. We got to get ready! They'll be here soon enough!" I shouted to wake the others. As they slowly tossed in their beds, groaning as their eyelids struggled to open, a knock came at the door.

"Travelers! You awake?! Are you...decent?!"

"Yes, we're...getting there!" I replied while watching my friends slowly plant their feet on the ground. The High Elf burst through the door, rushed across the room, and squeezed in to hug me like I was his long-lost son who finally returned home.

"Thank you. Thank the Heavens."

"Uhhh...you're welcome?" I hadn't the slightest idea why he was thanking me.

"You healed Malfae!" he said joyously.

"Oh. Yes. It wasn't a problem, though she seems to be a bit upset about it."

"Ah. You see, she's just bitter about...*uhhh*...almost being killed. I forgot to mention she is my baby sister. Who also happens to be the greatest warrior Zynthia has ever seen."

"I thought there was a resemblance there," Miri said.

"Yes. See, while I was preparing to one day take the throne, Malfae grew jealous as a child, not being treated the same or given the same responsibility, and so on. A bit unfair, yes, but it is how the kingdom works for a future king," he said as he stared intently at the flame inside the fireplace and cleared his throat. "So, she chose the path of war and training others for battle. She dedicated her life to it, with much success, I might add. Which is probably why she reacted the way she did about the whole situation," he explained.

"I guess that makes sense," I replied.

"Feeling as if she let everyone down during the fight because she was indisposed for part of it. I'm sure she fought well, but I can see your point." The king stood on his feet, headed towards the door, and said, "Now, if you would be so kind, there is something I must show you. You're all welcome."

High Elf Ralcord escorted us through the training room in the basement where the Ranger Brigade had been preparing for the next round of fighting. We reached a wall at the far end of the room, which held two torches at each corner. Ralcord suspiciously walked to the torch hanging on the left and scanned the room. Noticing the soldiers weren't paying attention to us, he grabbed the torch and pulled it slightly downward, creating a small *"clank"* noise behind the wall.

"Ah. I love doing that," Ralcord chuckled. A section of the wall turned slightly, creating an opening to walk through. "You first, Torren," Ralcord said, gesturing his hand outward.

"Uhhh. Okay." I was confused but went on anyway.

"Quickly now, everyone. Go. Go. Go. Good. Good." The High Elf had excitement in his voice while he hurried all of us to the dark room.

"I can't see anything in here. Wh—where are we, sir?" Cormac said.

"Torren, would you be so kind?" I waited a second for Ralcord to finish, but after a moment of silence, I realized what he meant. I held my hand out to illuminate the room, and something caught all of our attention. The light was reflecting off a small object on the opposite side of the room.

"What is that? Torren, make it brighter."

"Sorry, Miri, I was just being cautious. We don't know what's in here."

"Surely you wouldn't think I'd put you in any sort of danger, do you?" Ralcord asked.

"Well, no, but I've seen a lot of surprises these past few days," I replied. As we walked toward the glowing object, Ralcord started to explain.

"By now, I'm sure you know some of the history of the cloaks, your mother and her sister. You see, the day your mother and aunt discovered the orb, instead of leaving in shock, your mother marveled for a moment at the broken pieces scattered on the ground. This piece here," he pointed. "Your mother was drawn to it, so she decided to hold on to it." The piece was surprisingly smooth looking and had a certain glow to it that made my heart burst with excitement. You'd expect it to be at least a little more rigid or cracked, but besides a couple of pointy edges around the outside of the tiny white-colored jewel, it was pretty much flawless.

"Once the war started, my father suggested she wield a weapon to better protect herself. And as you know, your mother is not too fond of sharp, pointy objects made to harm someone," the High Elf said. "Much to her liking, she found a thick branch in the forest while spying on the enemy. With much care, and little time, she beautifully and flawlessly made this staff and placed the jewel from the broken orb."

"But would that break pretty easy while battling a werewolf?" Kyna asked.

"You would think so, but somehow or another, your mother's craftsmanship is nearly indestructible," Ralcord replied.

"Hmm. I mean, she always made little trinkets and wooden chests that seemed to never break. But no one ever questioned her about it that I remember," I stated.

"Torren, I am sorry for all the lies, the secrets in your life, but you have to understand it was all for the best." Ralcord could sense my emotions of confusion and frustration. There were a lot of things that still didn't quite make sense, but I know they were doing what they believed to be best for the kingdom, for me. And I wasn't about to open that can of worms again and feed the emotions. That would only make matters worse.

"Well, go on. Pick it up," Aevin said excitedly. We were all curious to see what would happen when I touched it. I looked over at the High Elf.

He grinned and nodded his head to say, "Yes, do it. Pick up the staff." As I reached out my hand, it was as if it called to me, greeting me as a friend. The feeling I got was something not of this world. The jewel at the top of the staff gleamed brighter as my hand got closer, and once I finally grasped the beautifully sculpted wood, the entire staff illuminated with a majestic glow from bottom to top. The jewel shined like the brightest star in the night sky, and I felt the light with more intensity than ever. The jaws of everyone in the room dropped to the floor, except for the High Elf; he was smiling from ear to ear with a certain twinkle in his eyes. The staff and I were connected somehow. I could feel the power flowing through it and into my blood.

"We call it the Staff of Lux. Meaning the light. You ever wonder where your family name comes from, Torren? Luxmin?" Ralcord asked, raising an eyebrow.

Everyone looked at me blankly as I pondered the king's question. And then it hit. I couldn't believe it took me so long to piece it together.

"So, my family, on my mother's side at least, are born to be healers? Well, not everyone, but you know what I'm saying."

"Correct. For years and years, your family has birthed healers, those who carry the light. Their power manifested through the years, evolving and becoming stronger. And you are the next one in line. Well, you and Jordiah. Before your mother and her sister, there had only been one healer at a given time. And now, with you and Jordiah, we have two once again. It's said to see his be used in such a dark manner. I can't say I blame him, though. Having his mother and father taken from him at such a young age and trained to despise our kind." Ralcord paused for a moment as he walked to the entrance. "If you choose to have children, they may or may not carry the light with them, and so on and so on. But I would bet that both your children would possess the ability. Though, only time will tell," the High Elf said.

My friends and I followed him to the door, and I was piecing together all the information I'd learned on this adventure. Things were starting to make more sense now.

Ralcord continued, "Jordiah's mother was the very first and only elf that we know of to have mated with a different race. The kingdom frowned upon members mating outside their own kind and cast her out because she was unwilling to leave Alpha Conri. And, of course, you know the rest." Everything was running through my mind like a whirlwind of words and pictures all tangled together. This war between our kinds had to end, but how? The fate of the kingdom was in our hands. The thought of dread began to form a pit in my stomach, like a rock weighing my insides down.

"Hey, you okay, Torren?" Miri must have noticed the alarming look on my face.

"I am. I jus—I just need to plan for tonight. Surely, we can't just wipe them all out or vice versa. There needs to be another way, a peaceful solution, to end this," I said as we passed through the secret door.

We marched back upstairs to a balcony hanging over the courtyard at the back of the castle. Glittered with a variety of colors, it sort of sprung a feeling of hope inside me, even with the dreadful feeling still gripping my insides. Miri walked to my side, gazed out to the courtyard, let out a contented sigh, and very gently placed her hand in mine as I laid her head on my shoulder. Not something I'd see as being very comfortable for her as she was slightly taller than me. My eyes opened wide with shock, but not a scared shock, more of a "well, this is unexpected, but nice" kind of shock. I decided to lay my head upon hers as we stood in silence.

"I..." Miri sighed and lifted her head, shifting her eyes to mine. "I love you, Torren." My heart grew, swelling with cheer. Part of me felt the longing to always be with her and knew she felt the same. But the biggest part of me would always say, "She could never love you that way. She deserves someone like Lorcan, who was smart, charming, and skilled." I must have been silent for too long, thinking of all the feelings I was going through because her smile started to turn into a sad glare.

"I love you, too," I said hastily. "I love you, too, Miri." I smiled and gazed into her beautiful blue eyes. We slowly began shifting our faces closer, and just before our lips were about to meet...

"Hey, guys, are you coming?" Cormac interrupted.

Me and Miri cleared our throats and took a step back.

"Uhh. Yeah. Yeah. Be right there. Right behind you," we said, skittish.

"Well, come on." We followed him back to our quarters, where the others were preparing for what would come very, very soon. The battle for Zynthia and its people. Life or death. I scanned the room, observing my friends, thinking back to our time growing up together and the adventures that we recently had gone through. They were more than just friends; they were my family. And tonight may be our last time together.

CHAPTER 11

Battle Number Two

Disclaimer: Please be advised that the following chapter contains scenes of violence that involve descriptions of harm and death to both people and animals. Reader discretion is strongly advised.

The sun had set, and there was a slight breeze flowing through the kingdom. I stood on the balcony where Miri and I had confessed our love to one another and stared up at the sky, gazing at the moon. Beautiful and majestic, even though it fueled our enemy with the power of transformation, speed, and strength. Turning them into bloodthirsty killing machines who loved to snack on elves. Regardless of what was about to happen, I was serene in the moment as the stars glistened in the sky, shining ever so brightly. I always found myself getting lost in the light as it shined through the darkest places, like the night sky or secret tunnels underneath the villages. *I hope everyone down there is safe. How are they on food? Should we send someone there to check on them?* My calm mind quickly turned to worry. I couldn't stop thinking that they would be helpless in the tunnels, especially if Jordiah and his pack caught even the slightest scent. Suddenly, I noticed the animals in the kingdom had scattered and grown silent. No barking dogs, no playful nickering from the horses or unicorns. I decided to walk around to get a look at Aurora and her foals. I stormed through the quarter's door, startling my peers.

"What is it, Torren?" Kyna asked. I ignored the question and hastily made my way to the window. Looking down, I noticed Aurora and her young ones were nervously pawing the ground and letting out quite unsettled nickers.

"Guys, it's time. They're here."

The others rushed to the window to get a quick look. "Where? I don't see them," Lorcan said.

"You can't see them, but...just quiet for a moment. You feel that?" They all stood in silence, trying to sense the air around us. It was filled with ominous fear and reeked of wet dogs.

"Keela, tell the king to be ready. Tell him it's time," Kyna instructed her sister. Keela stormed out of the room in a flash, and my only thought was, *I hope she isn't too flustered and forgets what to say or gets lost looking for him.* The rest of us continued to get ready, gathering our weapons and some prep drills before the fighting started. I grabbed my staff and rushed outside to Aurora.

I stood next to her, grazed my hand through her hair, and said, "Hey, girl. I know, it's about to get ugly. We'll be okay, I promise. I think." I didn't know what was about to transpire nor how I would protect her babies. This may be extremely ugly and deadly. I was determined that there had to be another way to settle this, but nothing useful actually came to mind.

"We have to trust each other tonight. It's the only way we both make it out alive," I said softly. "I have a secret to you, though. Me and Miri said, 'I love you' to each other." Aurora neighed with glee, jumping back on her hind legs. It was amazing that she seemed to understand what I was saying. "So, if we could, you know, do our best to keep her safe, maybe we will end up married someday? Who knows, though. But in all seriousness, we need to do our best to protect everyone." I went over to Aurora's foals to untie them, hoping they would run off to a safe place, but Aurora pulled at my cloak to stop me.

"You want them to stay? What if they get hurt?" Aurora shook her head from side to side and then pressed her nose against my chest. "You have a lot of faith in me, don't you, girl?" I pressed my head against hers and freed them from the post.

In the main corridor of the castle, I ran into Malfae and the Ranger Brigade.

"Torren, where you going? Where are you coming from?" the leader said with an uneasy tone.

"I was just with Aurora and her foals," I replied, realizing that her babies still didn't have names.

"Well, now you're coming with us. Where are your friends?"

"In the quarters, waiting."

I was soon informed that was the wrong answer as Malfae replied with, "Waiting? They should be preparing for battle. Not sitting on their rears waiting."

"I misspoke, is all. They are preparing."

"Good. Gather them and meet us at the gate. The battle will begin soon. Our hope is to keep them from reaching inside the kingdom walls."

"Like you attempted before?" I said; again, it was the wrong answer. I should realize what I'm implying before I let the words escape. "I didn't mean it in an offensive wa—"

Before I could finish my sentence, Malfae pushed past me, with the Rangers following behind her. I reached the quarters and informed them of what Malfae requested. Before leaving the room, I pulled Miri to the side and grabbed her hands in mine; no words would come out.

"What is it, Torren?" I stuttered for a moment. I couldn't realize why this was so hard. I wanted to say something, but nothing came to mind. Finally, Miri giggled and pulled me into her, giving me the tightest hug I've ever had, and whispered, "I know. We will be fine. Just have faith." We quickly shuffled to our friends and went to meet Malfae and the Rangers.

At the front gate, everyone was waiting on orders. It was quiet, almost too quiet for my own comfort. Aurora and her foal followed behind us but seemed calmer than earlier. Malfae raised her right fist in the air, and the gate guard opened the doors, but not fully. In columns of four, we marched outside the walls, heads held high, with our hearts and minds bearing the weight of the kingdom and its people. Much like the first battle, civilians picked up weapons in preparation, but they were ordered to stay inside the walls along with a few teams of Eru Psyawla warriors. Once everyone was outside the gate, we formed a defensive stance, waiting for the bloodthirsty wolves to emerge from the woodvine. Time seemed to stand still. It felt like we had waited forever, when really it had only been a few minutes. I was anxious to end this, but if it didn't start, what would that mean? Were we worrying and preparing for nothing? Surely, Jordiah wouldn't forfeit the fight. He wanted this too much unless his mate died. How much more pain could one person endure? The silence and waiting were starting to eat away at me. It just felt...awkward standing there, but the Rangers were laser-focused, determined. Situated near the middle of the group, we felt somewhat shielded. For most of my friends, that was satisfying. As for me, I found it a bit cowardly, especially given my newfound power. I started playing different scenarios in my head: Jordiah and his pack running from the tree line, stopping just before meeting us, and then we talked about the issues and ended the fighting. An unlikely event, but peaceful. On the other hand, and the most likely to occur, he attacked head-on, creating a bloodbath out of both parties. *Either way, I have to be ready, but the truth is, I am scared out of my mind.*

After all the waiting and anticipation, an *Ahh—wooooo* came from the forest ahead of us, sparking Malfae to say, "Everybody ready!"

The Rangers around us quickly jumped to a fighting stance, readying their weapons. More howls and growls echoed from the front, getting closer and closer. It was almost as if they wanted us to know they were coming. The soldiers in the rear of the formation stood guard, watching for a surprise from behind. The atmosphere was tense and fearful as we were about to meet the enemy for a second time, and the first fight wasn't as any of us expected. Suddenly, Jordiah peered through the line of trees, floating in the air, and transformed.

I thought to myself, *Well, if he can float, I should be able to.* I closed my eyes and tried to feel the air around me, feeling it lift me above the crowd. My staff, as well as my eyes, began to glow as I opened them, and suddenly I was in the air. The crowd gasped in awe at my hovering as I pushed closer to the front, unsteady.

"New to this, I see, cousin," Jordiah said jokingly.

"Fairly, but I believe I got a good handle on the situation," I replied. And without hesitation, Jordiah fired a beam straight at me, which I dodged, but not gracefully at all. I went head over heels, tumbling through the air as if I were doing cartwheels. The pack of wolves laughed at the sight but were quickly thrown afoot as Malfae and the Rangers began to attack.

Once I gathered myself, I slid side to side in the air, trying to get acquainted with the feeling. Noticing the fight had begun, I scanned the battlefield for Miri and my friends. I spotted her right when Jordiah tackled me out of the air.

"First rule of war, always keep your eyes on the enemy, Torren." Right as we hit the ground, Jordiah started swinging his fist right to my face, landing only one blow before I blasted him off with a fierce ray of light. And out of the darkness came screams from inside the kingdom walls. A surprise attack planned by Jordiah and his pack.

I called to Miri, "Hey, we need to go help."

"But Jordiah is here. Once he's killed, this useless battle ends," Kyna replied as she drove her sword through one of the wolves. I floated back up to air and noticed that Malfae had Jordiah distracted, so I went to Miri, Lorcan, and Aevin, who were handling their own surprisingly well.

"The first round was good practice, I see."

"Yeah, I must prefer to be at a distance."

"What's wrong, Lorcan? Afraid to get your hands dirty?" Kyna, being chased by a werewolf, heard Lorcan's comment, turned, and jumped over the beast as Keela decapitated it.

"Nice work, sisters."

"Aevin, Cormac, Kyna, you three go back to the castle and assist. If we can, one of us will come check on you in a bit. Hopefully, this won't take long."

The battle was not as intense as I had thought. The wolves seemed a bit off, even with the moon giving them power. Regardless, the fighting was exhausting. And not just physically; the bloodshed, the death, was mentally and emotionally trying. I didn't want to harm anyone. I never have. I fought as hard as I could, pushing back the beast and using my staff to melee. I tried to hold back on my power, knowing it would tire me more quickly the more I used it. Finally, I was face to face with Jordiah again.

"Not too bad, I see." He grinned, death and agony behind both of us.

"How can you smile at this?" I asked.

"At what? Fighting for what belongs to us? We were outcasts because of love!" Jordiah shouted. "Do you know what that feels like?"

I glanced over to Miri at the sound of his words.

"Jordiah, I don't know what that is like. But that wasn't you, it wasn't your time. I know, they were your parents, and that has to hurt. But this—the killing, the fighting, it solves nothing. It won't bring them back," I tried to reason. His eyes glowed a deep red and purple, adding to the eerie figure he already was. "I have a surprise for my dear cousin. Maybe you'll soon know what it's like. To feel as I feel." Jordiah growled as one of his pack members dragged my parents out of the tree line.

"Mom! Dad!" I yelled in desperation. "Don't lay a hand on them!" I demanded, noticing they were already wounded.

Jordiah took hold of my mother and pushed his face to hers.

"This one here, Aunt Ailbhe, is the one responsible, isn't that right?" My half-blood cousin cried.

"Jordiah, she was my sister. I didn't want to kill her, but she was killing everyone in her path. She was revenge-stricken. She had to be stopped. We tried to reason with her, bu—" Jordiah interrupted her by piercing his long, sharp claws through her neck. And then quickly through my father's heart.

"Nooooo!" I yelled and made an attempt to reach them to heal them, but three of Jordiah's pack members held me back. I fell to my knees and began to sob, noticing Miri fighting Luna Bella, using her telekinesis to evade the werewolf, when suddenly, a wolf came from behind her, thrusting his claws into her back. Filled with anger and sadness, I slammed my fist to the ground, and a wave of light burst outward in every direction, causing everyone on the battlefield to be thrown to the ground. I glided to the air over to Miri, thankfully still alive. I looked into her eyes, slowly seeming to fade as she gasped for air, and kissed her forehead. A tear rolled down my cheek. Her body shimmered with light, brighter than the brightest star in the sky, and she began to moan and groan in pain. Everyone who saw the event gasped in awe as they were frozen on the battlefield. It was so silent, you could hear a pin drop. Miri sighed a sigh of relief after the kiss healed her wounds and looked up at me.

"Thank you. I—I'm sorry, Torren."

I stood to my feet, staff in hand, and light grazed my eyes around me, scalding. I floated to the sky, looking above the kingdom. There, I saw the people of Zynthia putting up a good fight and driving the wolves back to the front gate, so I didn't interfere with them. The werewolves lying on the field shakenly stood to their feet and let out an *Aahhhh-woooooo* as three of them charged at me like crazed, bloodthirsty demons, growling and snarling with every step. I wasn't so high up that they couldn't jump and grab me, which, at this point, I wanted them to try. I glanced at my parent's lifeless bodies; I should've tried to save them somehow, but when Miri got hurt, I couldn't think of anyone else but her. I changed my direction back at the wolves charging me and held out my staff. A giant, bright white beam shot out from the jewel of the staff, almost evaporating the charging beast.

Malfae could be heard yelling, "That's it, Torren! Show them what you're made of!"

I shrugged off the comment; I didn't want anything else in my head. I wanted them to pay. I wanted them to burn for what they did to my parents, to Miri. I came back to the ground as the shocking blow I just dealt and continued to display my rage to the wolves on the ground. I paused and whistled for Aurora, but she nervously ran into the forest, her foals following behind.

"Fine. I'll do this myself," I muttered. I could feel my power beginning to drain, but I was still feeling electric. All around me, my peers fought off the pack; some died or were wounded. I walked around healing those that I could, but my ultimate goal was to reach Jordiah, who had fled once I shocked everyone by disintegrating some of his friends. He was nowhere to be found.

The pack had made a strong move toward the kingdom wall. Some, like before, began jumping the wall to help their brothers and sisters struggling to gain ground inside. Lorcan was in his natural fighting position, far away and slightly above the battlegrounds, picking off as many as he could with his bow and arrows. I scanned the battlefield and spotted Lorcan from afar and flew over to him.

"Why didn't you stop him? Why did you just let him kill my parents? You could see the whole thing from here."

"Torren, I—" He let an arrow fly past me, straight into a wolf lunging at me. "I couldn't get a good shot. He used you as a cover. If I took the shot, I risked hitting you, possibly your mother. I couldn't do that," Lorcan explained.

"I'm sorry," I grunted and glided off, charging the battlefield, looking for Miri, and there she was, aided by Kyna and Cormac. I was so hurt, so torn. My parents were everything to me, and to watch them die like that in front of me nearly destroyed me.

"Torren, calm down. You don't want to keep doing this. You can't keep doing this," Miri yelled as I approached them. I spotted Jordiah and a few of his pack jumping over the wall.

Ignoring Miri's comment, "Come on," I said. "We need to go inside the kingdom and help." I grabbed her and followed them to the front gate. "Hope you don't mind."

"Are you kidding? This is fun! But seriously, you need to calm down. I understand you're hurt, but this is—this is not right, Torren." She wrapped her arms around me in a sympathetic squeeze and whispered, "I'm sorry," as we flew over the kingdom. Me floating around seemed effortless, but in reality, it was exceedingly tiresome. I was beginning to feel exhausted. I had to land to gather my strength, to rest, but it was crawling with Jordiah's army and fighting soldiers.

"Are you all right, Torren?"

"Yes, Mir, I'm fine."

I wasn't fine, and she could sense it. She could tell by the rhythm of my heartbeat as it beat against her head lying on my chest.

Finally, I drunkenly glided atop a ledge hanging from a tower window. A very slim ledge at that. I struggled to guide Miri through the window of the tower as I awkwardly lifted her and my staff over the window seal, nearly falling to the ground below.

"I need something—some food...or something," I muttered. "I feel so tired, so weak."

"Lucky for you." Miri reached for a bag in the corner of the tower and pulled out a boot, a shirt, and a women's skirt. "I really thought there would be food in that bad. Why would a bag of clothes be all the way up here?"

"Do we really want to know the answer to that?" I remarked as I slumped my head over my knees. "I just need to rest."

"Torren, you think all that...anger took all your energy?" she asked softly.

"I don't want to talk about that. I have a right to be mad. To be upset."

"I'm not saying you don't. I'm just saying..." Miri paused for a moment. "I'm just saying that rage, revenge, and hate, isn't that what turned your aunt away from the light? I just don't want to see that happen to you. You have to hold onto the light."

I leaned over and laid my head on Miri's shoulder. It was soothing; the connection we had, the feeling she gave me while sitting next to me, the way she looked at me in any situation with cheer and glee. Except when I went on my slight frenzy moments ago. Still, she found a way to show her care towards me. My heart was still burdened with sadness as I began to sob in Miri's arms.

Jordiah and his pack had made a well-defined march towards the castle, regaining his strength as the night grew darker and colder. The moon shined bright in the sky, and not a cloud was in sight to hide the power it fed to the wolves. Fire and smoke quickly began filling the air as the pack torched their way through the Eru Psyawla, destroying anyone and anything who stood in their way. Screams and cries echoed like songs of the damned through the darkness. It was terrifying, and me being mentally bound in a tower with Miri made my guilt begin to grow. I had to help, somehow, but my strength was just starting to rebuild. I was in no shape, mentally or physically, to fight.

"I'll be right back," Miri said as she stood up and headed towards the door.

"Wait," I shouted hastily, hoping she would just stay with me a little longer.

"We can't just stay here," she stated as she peered through the window. "They're almost to the castle. The moon is too powerful tonight. It's like a—a...a super moon now or something. I need to find you some food, something to give you strength."

She stormed through the door and headed down the staircase. I looked through the window for a brief moment, seeing the destruction and chaos below. The sight disgusted me; it formed a pit in my stomach. I quickly hunched back down. I couldn't bear to see any more bloodshed.

Miri scared the life out of me when she busted through the door, holding a sack of berries and nuts she found scattered at the bottom of the tower.

"You were gone a while."

"I couldn't force myself to leave the tower, but thankfully, I found these spread out on the floor at the bottom. Someone must have dropped it running away or something," she said as she handed me the bag. It wasn't a full meal, but it definitely hit the spot, and I was thankful that she wasn't captured by a member of the pack.

"Thank you," I said.

"So, feeling better."

"Yeah, but still not a hundred percent. But I feel we don't have time to waste on that. We've already been here too long, and Jordiah is getting stronger, as you pointed out already," I said, hanging my head in shame.

"Hey, don't do that. You couldn't help it, Torren. You had to regain your power." As Miri spoke, I got lost in the shimmer of the jewel on my staff. Her voice began fading in the background as the jewel seemed brighter and brighter. And suddenly, I knew what to do.

"Your par—"

"The jewel has the power in it, right?" I cut Miri off.

"I—What? I guess it does. Were you listening to what I was saying?"

"Not to be rude, but not really. But if it has the power that enhanced the cloaks, wouldn't it make sense it would…recharge me?" I turned from the jewel and looked at Miri.

"Yeah. Yeah, I suppose that could work." I lit a small glare of light in my palm, and as the stone on my staff began to glow, I touched my hand to it, gripping it as if I were trying to pull it from the wooden fibers it was constructed to. Immediately, the light in my hand grew brighter, and I could feel the light in my veins once more, much like the first time I touched the staff. And with my regained strength, Miri and I hiked down the tower and headed for the castle.

CHAPTER 12

A Field of Dead Flowers

We ran into Lorcan, Cormac, and Kyna across the street from the castle. They were in an intense battle with a group of bloodthirsty wolves, struggling to stay on their feet. Cormac had been wounded on his left shoulder and was finding it hard to hold his sword. We could tell that Kyna was winded and losing her strength; still, she was fending off the beasts with ferocity. Lorcan seemed uncomfortable not being perched in a tree or in a tower using his bow; he was fighting awkwardly with a sword.

"Where are the others?" I said as I ran in and hit one of the werewolves with my staff, creating a wave of light that stunned the others. Miri used her telekinesis to keep the wolves at bay long enough for Lorcan to explain that Aevin and Keela had gone with Malfae inside the castle wall, as well as get a breather for a moment.

Miri let loose her power and said, "I can't hold them," frantically as she ran back toward us. The wolves howled and charged at us with death in their eyes. One lunged past Kyna, swiping its paw at her face.

"*Ahhh*," she grunted in pain as the beast inflected a nasty gash across her right cheek. She quickly turned and threw her dagger right through its heart. As she ran over to retrieve the dagger from the beast, another wolf ran straight for her, noticing she was unaware. I took my staff and shot a beam in its direction, missing it. The light was close enough and bright enough to throw it off balance and blind it long enough for Kyna to pull her dagger and rejoin the fight.

"Never turn your back on the enemy, Kyna," Lorcan said, running, ducking and dodging a wolf. We continued fighting for a short while, and then I got an idea.

"Everyone, close your eyes!" I shouted as I held my staff in the air, emitting a giant glare of light, blinding the enemy long enough for us to evade them. "We need to get to the castle or find Jordiah first," I said as we ran to an alley away from the beast.

In the abandoned alley way, we found a useful substance to mask our scent, Freesia flowers. Safe for the moment, I took the time to tend to my wounded friends, though Kyna stubbornly tried to evade my attempts to heal her.

"No. Don't waste your energy. My wounds are not life-threatening; I'll be fine." I attempted to persuade her but eventually gave in and let her be.

"We will rest here for a short time, gather our wits and strength. Maybe come up with a plan," I whispered.

"Plan how? We don't know what we're doing. We're just here, and Malfae is out there somewhere in the castle. She makes the plans. Not us," Kyna said.

"It wouldn't hurt to figure out what to do next, Kyna," Miri defended. "It's better than going in blindly, most times. That's all he's saying."

"Fine. I suppose that's true, but what do we do? None of us really know what we're doing." Kyna admitted in exasperation, raising her voice slightly and shrugging her shoulders. "Shhh. Quiet," I whispered. "Are you trying to draw them here?"

"I'm sorry. I'm just...on edge. Maybe a little scared. I thought they wouldn't be as strong this time, but somehow, they seem more powerful."

We hunched down in the alley for a while trying to formulate a plan, unsuccessfully. We hadn't the slightest clue what to do. Cormac eventually started rummaging through bags and broken vendor tables in search of some food. It had been a long night, we were hungry, tired, and just flat-out ready for all this to be over. Unfortunately, his rummaging was quite noisy and attracted some unwanted attention from some nearby strangers.

From around the corner appeared a slender figure, followed by another about the same size. We were stricken with fear, worried that we may be spotted. If wolves found us, they would have a field day realizing we were cornered in this dead-end alley. Definitely not the most advantageous situation for any of us to be in. Sure, they were only two, but two wolves could easily double or triple with a quick warning howl. Once the figures stepped a little closer and further into the light, my heart warmed as I realized who the shadowy figures belonged to, though sadness tugged at me to see them alone.

"Beatrix?" I asked, my voice low. The little girls gasped in shock and nearly fell back.

"Ye—yes. Who's there?" she whimpered.

I stepped out of the dark shadow and said, "It's me, Torren, from earlier. Remember me?" I asked as I lowered my hood. The girl smiled in relief and let out a slight giggle as she ran toward me with her arms open wide. She wrapped her arms around me in a great big bear hug, nearly squeezing the breath out of me. Then, Beatrix began to cry.

"What's the matter, Be?"

"Our parents, they—they..." she sniffled and wiped her eyes, "They're dead. It's just me and my little sister, Brittany. I don't know what to do or where to go."

I looked back at my friends, grief and anger evident in my eyes.

"Don't worry. You can stay with us for the time being. Soon, we will head toward the castle. They should have food there, and I'm sure there's a place inside where the wolves won't find you," I said with as much confidence as I could manage, adding more gently, "I'm sorry about your mom and dad. They seemed like great people." She and her sister squeezed in and hugged me once again.

My friends and I escorted the sisters, keeping them between us as we sneakily hiked to the castle. The wolves were everywhere, leaving destruction in their wake as they scavenged the kingdom, searching for survivors. We could hear people inside the castle wall panicking as the wolves made their way over. The night had been long and extremely tiresome. My anxiety built as the darkness grew colder and the fire created by the pack spread. They were relentless, furiously gaining the upper hand in the battle. We finally made our way to the castle wall, along the backside and out of sight, or so we thought.

"Aaooooow!" a wolf howled as it barreled toward us. Soon after, four more came around the corner.

"It's him!" one called and turned back. I imagined it was going to inform Jordiah of our location. We had to stay and fight and risk a handful more wolves showing up or take a chance on running.

"Lorcan, use your bow," Kyna said. Lorcan pulled back three arrows and let them fly, piercing two of the wolves in the shoulder.

"Come on," I instructed as I turned and ran deeper into the kingdom, away from the castle. We made our way to an abandoned house, fortunately unlocked, and scrambled inside. It had already been ransacked by the pack, so we were hopeful they wouldn't search the house first.

"What now?" I said. "We can't get close to the wall without being spotted by them. Our friends need our help, but how can we help if we can't get in?" I added.

"Torren, I know it's hard, but we need to stay positive. Negativity solves nothing," Miri said. Cormac went off to another room as I went on a rant about how silly it was to attempt to enter the castle again. Even though Jordiah and his pack should have been weakened due to the Luna being wounded, which would cause Jordiah to be limited, the wolves somehow seemed stronger. Maybe it was Jordiah's determination to get revenge for Lorcan's arrow that nearly killed his love, or perhaps the power from the moon we underestimated. Either way, defeat loomed over the kingdom like a dark cloud just before a storm. We feared for what the future may bring, who would still be standing when this was all over.

"We can't keep wasting time, running, and hiding, regardless of the situation. If we sit and do nothing, the kingdom is surely doomed. If we fight, maybe we will hold them off until sunrise. By then, they would be transformed back to human, or in Jordiah's case, elf form and considerably weaker," I said, pacing the room.

"Torren, calm down. We're all worried. Kyna more so, her sister is inside, and we have no way to know if she's all right."

"Thanks a lot, Miri. I haven't thought much about it until now," Kyna replied abrasively.

Startlingly, Cormac stormed into the room, holding what seemed to be fur, a wolf's fur.

"I think I have an idea."

We hadn't the slightest clue why the abandoned house had skins and fur of wolves, but we knew we could somehow use it to our advantage, so we hoped. There were only three skins, so two of us would have to create a distraction for the ones wearing the disguises. The argument went as follows.

"I think since I found them, I should be able to wear them," Cormac stated. "True, you did find them, but I should wear one, being I am the one with the power of light. I am the one who should take out Jordiah."

"So, you think it's just because we don't have the power you possess that we couldn't take him? Is that what you're saying, Torren?"

"No, Kyna. Not at all. I'm just saying that it would be more of a fair fight, me versus him, than any of you versus him."

Kyna scoffed at my comment and walked to the other side of the room. She has always been a strong-willed woman. Not that there's anything wrong with that. Her and Miri were kind of similar. Only Miri was a bit more gentle hearted.

"Okay. Here's what we will do," Lorcan said. He's always been more of a leader than me. Just the last few days I've had to make some decisions that haven't come so easy for me. Normally, I hated deciding, planning what to do. The next steps to take. But in the last few days, it almost came naturally, except now. It was like the moon had magnified my anxiety to a new level of panic. I couldn't decide on anything. Only worry.

Lorcan continued, "Torren, Miri, and Cormac will wear the fur while Kyna and I create a distraction."

"What about the sisters?" I asked. Lorcan seemed to ponder the question for a good moment while occasionally gazing at the young children and back to the front door.

"It's too dangerous for them to come with Kyna and myself. They either stay hidden here, or you can pretend you captured them?" Lorcan suggested.

The sisters whispered to one another, then turned towards me.

"We want to go with Torren."

"Well, I suppose I take them, then."

Disguised with the revolting scent of the wolves' fur, Mir, Cormac, and I covertly exited the abandoned house, with Beatrix and her sister snuck away close to us. While Kyna and Lorcan followed slightly behind. We managed to make it across the road from the main gate without spotting a wolf. Unfortunately, the pack and members of the Ranger Brigade were still battling in plain sight. Lorcan decided to sneak around the back side of the castle wall with Kyna. He instructed the rest of us to count to thirty or wait until we heard them fighting to push along the side of the wall and attempt to jump over. We counted to twenty-two and finally heard them moaning and grunting as they fought off a few members of the pack. Me, Miri, and Cormac made our move, using our disguises to run past the enemy at the front gate. The fur was itchy and very unpleasant to smell, but it worked! While it was similar in color and smell to the werewolves, it didn't cover us completely. If one of the pack members examined enough, they would easily tell we weren't real werewolves. Luckily, they were distracted with fighting the Rangers. Standing alongside the wall, we could hear people struggling to fend off the enemy on the other side. We decided to hunch behind a tree next to the wall and wait for the commotion to stop. If we went over now, we could be attacked by our own kind and the enemy. I thought about how terrible it would be to make it this far in the night and be so close to the castle, then be killed by one of my own kind as they mistook me for a wolf.

After a short moment, the fighting stopped, and we heard an elf yell out, "Aha! Yes! Run, you cowards," as the foes were heard scrambling away, jumping the castle wall right over the three of us. We sat next to the tree, frozen in fear, hoping the wolves wouldn't smell us being so close.

As they walked away, we could hear their conversation, "Nomad, these elves are foolish and weak. Why did we run?"

"Johnathan, we did our job; we distracted them long enough. They put up a good fight; we wouldn't have killed them all. Jordiah is making his move soon, so we need to be ready."

Making his move? What was his plan? What game was he playing? I couldn't help but wonder as I scanned the perimeter thoroughly for any sign of bystanders and listened carefully for noise coming from the opposite side of the wall. Once I felt the area was safe, I floated over the wall, carrying Miri and Beatrix, then proceeded to help Cormac and Brittany over the wall. There was chaos, sheer terror inside the castle wall and all in the courtyard. There was an elf-made wall surrounding the outside of the castle to keep the beasts at bay. We scoured the surrounding area, waiting for our best chance to make it into the castle. Off to our left, toward the backside of the castle, we saw two werewolves jump the wall holding Lorcan and Kyna. They were squirming viciously, so at least they were still alive.

"Hey, look over there." I pointed at our captured friends.

"It's Lorcan and Kyna. We need to help them. Have you seen any sign of Keela or Aevin? Malfae?" I whispered softly. Miri shook her head no. This is when I wished Lorcan were here. He'd know what to do. He'd have a plan. I stumbled through thoughts and ideas to rescue our friends, all while keeping the girls safe, and finally, I said, "Okay, you three head toward the castle steps. Don't forget that you look and smell like a wolf, so take down your disguise just before you reach the guards. I'll go free our friends, I hope."

I had slight doubts about the plan, but it was the best I could come up with. I knew if the girls made it inside the castle, they would have the best chance of survival, and that included Miri. On the other hand, Miri is pretty scrappy, even though she doesn't look like it or seem the type, but she was very strong and tactical, so she could be useful in aiding me to free Lorcan and Kyna. Just before splitting off, I reached for Miri and kissed her, causing her to blush as the little girls smiled and reacted with *"Oooo"* in sheer giggles.

"Once they are safe, I'll need you back there with me." Miri nodded her head, kissed me on the cheek, and sprinted toward the front of the castle.

"Hey!" I yelled as I discarded my disguise and held my staff out, aiming toward the wolves holding Lorcan and Kyna. It wasn't nearly as dramatic as it was in my head, I realized as three of the beasts began laughing.

"You think that little stick will keep us from eating your friends?" one said.

"We'll just have to see, won't we?" I replied confidently.

Lorcan and Kyna were seemingly stunned for the time being; I had to act quickly in order for them not to be snatched by another bystander wolf and killed. I quickly dodged the first wolf lunging at me, but a second beast managed to ram me in the side with its shoulder, sending me flying across the courtyard. I was rattled in my head as the pain shot through my ribs and up to my neck. I hesitated for a moment but quickly realized the situation as two foes blazed toward me like an angry fire. Just before they reached me, I firmly planted the bottom of my staff to the ground with a thunderous blow, dispersing a shockwave of light through the earth. The magnitude of power knocked the beasts back, rending them unconscious. Their bodies began shifting back to normal form as they lay there, sleeping unintentionally. I ran to my friends as quickly as I could and started to heal their wounded bodies. Just then, Jordiah swooped in and hit me with a surprising blow to my back.

"I've waited all night for this. Now the real fun begins, cousin," he snarled as he dramatically walked closer to me.

He kneeled by my side and smiled at me as I lay on the ground. "My power grows weaker as my mate slowly dies from the silver in her blood. You will die just as slowly. And then," he began to chuckle. "Then I'll take that jewel of yours for myself and kill all your friends." He stood on his feet and began kicking me repeatedly in my side, my stomach, my back. I was so beaten. Physically and mentally. I had failed. I had failed my friends and my family. I had failed Miri. The kingdom would be ruled by ruthless werewolves, and the elves who survived would have no life at all except to be slaves of Jordiah. In the distance I heard Miri cry out in a heartbroken scream as Jordiah went flying through the air. He was determined to make this take as long as possible, like he promised. Just like that, he was out of sight, and I feared what he was going to do next.

Miri ran to my side and said, "Torren, heal yourself. We don't have much longer. Heal yourself! Now!" I barely understood what was happening, what she was saying. My ears rang like whistles and bells singing tunes inside my head. Through the fog and pain, I finally comprehended the words she was speaking and grabbed the jewel on my staff. The power surged through me and healed my partially broken body. As I stood on my feet, I guided Miri to my side, squeezing her tightly against my body. Shortly after, Keela, Aevin, and Malfae joined us.

"Nice to see you again, Torren," Malfae said.

"Likewise," I replied. Keela ran to Lorcan and gave him a kiss.

"Are you okay?"

"I'll be fine, thanks to Torren."

"*Oh*, I almost forgot. Come here, you and Kyna." I gathered Lorcan and Kyna closer to me and continued to heal their bodies.

"Almost unfair, don't you think?" Lorcan said.

"I mean, I didn't ask to be a healer, but since I possess the power, why not use it, right?" I replied. "I'm just not sure how long I can keep this up."

"Feeling tired already, Torren?" Malfae said.

"Ehh, let's just finish this," I grunted.

Just like the beginning of the battle, elves and werewolves were face to face, squared against each other on either side of the courtyard. Bushes and flowers lay scattered on the ground, dying with no roots planted in the soil. I stared into Jordiah's cold, evil eyes and felt more than revenge. I felt sadness and loneliness. I felt desperation, wanting to be loved. To be remembered. Much of how I felt for most of my life.

Jordiah must have felt my gaze; he quickly muttered, "That's enough," howled, and the wolves charged at us like lightning. Jordiah knew he didn't have much longer before the sun would awaken, and the power from the moon would soon disappear, leaving him and his pack nearly defenseless against me and my power of light. The power of the moon was merely all that was keeping his mate alive, and Jordiah knew that. I felt it, too, as she charged by his side. Almost as if she were gasping for breath with every stride and fighting for her heart to keep beating. Just a moment passed, and the two sides collided for the most powerful and striking battle of the night. Jordiah didn't take to the air this time; he was content staying on the ground, which made me feel at ease. Fighting in the air had a certain sway that my head didn't take kindly to. Back and forth, round and round, we fought. Tumbling over, grappling, throwing, punching, kicking, you name it. The courtyard was blazing with chaos and rage as the king and queen watched from the balcony above. Their home, their people, were being destroyed right before them. It broke their hearts; still, they felt better staying inside this time and being the last line of defense to protect their son, which I couldn't blame them for; I would too if I were them. I used blasts of light to keep most of the attacks at bay, one by one or two by two, sometimes three at a time, charging me. Death was all around me, and I quickly realized the courtyard, the kingdom that once danced with life, was now a graveyard, cold and grey. Breathing the air of battle.

Malfae had managed to separate from the pack, trailing off in the opposite direction in hopes the wolves would be led away from the castle. Surprisingly, it worked; a group of wolves followed blindly into Malfae's trap as she lured them into a spring-loaded silver-netted trap, which suspended the wolves up in the air as they moaned in pain from the silver burning through their fur.

"Nice, but where was that earlier?" Lorcan asked.

"It malfunctioned. It wasn't our fault, but it worked this time, so all is forgiven," Keela replied, kissed Lorcan on the cheek, and continued battling a wolf. I, on the other hand, had to deal with Jordiah and Bella at the same time. Both were obnoxiously swinging their claws and butting me with their head. Most of their attacks I managed to defend, but they managed to land a few good ones on my shoulder, my back, and my leg. I countered with a few myself, using my staff to whack Bella across her side, the same side Lorcan pierced with an arrow, making her stumble to the ground with pain. She was slow to get up afterward, and Jordiah noticed her struggling. He charged at me in rage, and just before he bit a chuck out of my stomach, I slid to the side, holding my staff out for him to trip on. He was swift and wise enough to notice and jumped over my staff, hooking his head toward me and taking a bite of flesh from my arm.

"*Aahhhh*," I grunted in pain. I glanced at Bella. She was breathing but not in any condition to move. She just laid there. I looked back at the missing flesh from my arm, stared at Jordiah, and healed the wound. His smile quickly faded once he saw my flesh growing back. This only made him angrier as he charged at me once more. This time, I didn't dodge him. I barreled at him, determined to end this war before sunrise. As we collided, I could feel his claws attempt to sink through my skin, but I was aware enough to avoid the talons he carried. He was getting weaker by the minute. After a while, it almost didn't feel like a fair fight.

Jordiah doubled over; his breathing seemed labored. "Don't worry, dear cousin. This isn't over. You'll see." He looked at Bella once more. "You'll be okay, my love. I promise you. We will win this," he muttered.

I looked around at the courtyard turned battlefield. The wolves were beginning to struggle. Maybe it was the moonlight starting to fade, or maybe we found a new strength somehow. As I scanned over the bodies lying on the earth below me, I felt a sort of sadness in my heart that I hadn't felt in my entire life. A glimpse of the feeling I had earlier, sure, but this was more intense. I felt just as bad for Jordiah and his pack as I did for the elves. I couldn't understand why all the secrets, why we couldn't share this land, and what was so wrong with half-bloods in the kingdom. This war didn't make sense, and for me to be a part of it broke my heart even more. I looked over at Miri, fighting alongside our friends. You could see the pain in their faces. The war was scarring their hearts, all of our hearts. Even if we win this battle, we've lost the war that matters. I lowered my head in shame and fell to my knees with a tear running down my cheek. The battle fighting, the screaming, all the echoes of war seemed to go silent. I lifted my head and noticed everyone was staring at me. But I hadn't the, But I had no idea why, until I looked down at my hands and saw them glowing. The radiance swirled around me like the light from a star. I was merely shell-shocked at what had happened. The feeling inside me was that of a thousand broken hearts, all crying out for love, for healing. Crying for help.

I thought back to the vision I had the day I left Ms. Crosman's house, "Forgive, but do not forget. Cure the dark, but do not blind with light." And suddenly, I knew what to do. I stood on my feet and walked over to Bella.

"I'm sorry," I whispered.

Jordiah yelled "You get away from her, dirty elf!" As he ran toward me, I held my hand out, shining light from my palm that gently stopped him in his tracks.

"Wait. You'll see," I told him.

"Wha—What are you doing, Torren?" Malfae said angrily.

"Ending this war, but not with spilled blood," I said. "Bring the king and his wife," I commanded. "They need to see this."

I began to heal Bella. As she moaned and growled in pain, Jordiah grew impatient and frustrated, trying to charge at me, but the light that my body produced somehow created a force field around Bella and I, so he was unable to reach us.

Realizing his effort was pointless, he fell to his knees, crying out, "Why?! What are you doing to her?" as he began to weep. A moment passed, and the light around Bella and I started to fade. I heard gasps come from the crowd as Bella rose to her feet and walked over to Jordiah. She placed her arms around him, hugging him softly.

"I—I'm fine, my love. I'm alive," she said as she lifted his head towards hers and kissed him softly.

"I love you," Jordiah told Bella.

"What just happened?" Ralcord yelled from the balcony hanging over the courtyard. I looked up and floated above the crowd of people and stared at them for a moment.

"This is the end of the war," I shouted. "Both sides have wronged one another for far too long. We are supposed to be one. We are supposed to live amongst one another in peace. All this hate, all this death...it's nonsense. I myself have caused enough pain and blood for an entire lifetime." I began to shed a tear as I looked upon their faces. "They had a home, long ago, shared with our kind. And because of love, a love for a different kind, they were cast out, cursed." I looked in the direction of the king and his wife.

"How is that fair? In that one instance, it caused the death of my aunt, my mother and father, and countless more. It makes no sense."

"Torren, you misunderstand the situation, I believe. The war was started out of revenge," the High Elf stated.

"Revenge for what your father did to my aunt and his father," I exclaimed as I pointed towards Jordiah. "We can start a new life together, without revenge, without hate. Sure, we won't always get along. We're not perfect people. But the only way any of us win is together." I heard Aurora and her foals neighing and frolicking to the back side of the gate. She seemed pleased at what she was seeing, and I was excited to see her in good spirits and unharmed.

"Aurora, welcome back! Excuse me for a moment." I couldn't help but float down and greet her and the foals; I think she was happy, too. She galloped around cheerfully once she saw me moving towards her.

"Hey, girl. How are you? Where did you go, huh?" I said as I petted her nose. "I'm sorry I sort of lost my temper earlier. Forgive me, will you?" Aurora neighed and pressed her head against mine.

"Apologies for the interruption," I said once I moved back toward the crowd. "Jordiah, I forgive you for what pain you have caused. I am hurt by my parents' fate, for all this you see around us, but I forgive you. I, too, want to apologize for the pain, not only I have caused, but for the pain and torment the kingdom has cause you and your pack," I said as I hugged Jordiah.

"I—I ca—" He tried to fight but was overtaken by an overwhelming sensation in his heart as he looked into Bella's eyes, realizing that I had healed her even after what he had done. He grew speechless and began to cry on my shoulder.

"I'm sorry," he began to mutter repeatedly.

"As for you, High Elf, Ralcord," I stared the king down from below and shouted. "I forgive you for the lies and the secrets. I also apologize for my ignorance and stubbornness on the matter. I know you were only trying to protect the kingdom the way you were taught and saw fit. But excluding and forbidding others just because they look different or," I leaned over to Jordiah and wafted his scent to my nose, trying to lighten the mood a little with some humor, "smell different, are not what will hold this kingdom together," I said. "It would only tear us apart. And I believe this was a rather good example of that; look around!" I said, waving my hand out from my chest to my side. The king and his wife looked at their kingdom, the destruction in all its dismay, as their heads hung low and tears filled their eyes.

"Let it be!" Ralcord started after a moment of crying. "Let it be declared, if Jordiah and his pack agree, that the Kingdom of Zynthia shall be their home as much as it is ours. That he and his pack will be given equal rights and love from the kingdom and its people, from now until ever!"

Jordiah looked around at his pack and back up at the king and said, "Thank you, High Elf Ralcord, but we accept under only one condition."

CHAPTER 13

New Beginnings

The sun rose with a joyous light gleaming across the sky, shining on all of Zynthia. It was a beautiful start to a new day for the kingdom and its people. We wanted to celebrate the new alliance, but everyone was so exhausted and beaten that we couldn't bear to take on any new excitement until after a good meal and some rest.

"That was something, Torren," Malfae muttered as she walked up beside me and Miri.

"Um. Thanks, I think."

"You know, I never would have thought that war could be ended in such a peaceful manner, but you proved me wrong. I was downright mad at first with how you handled it. I wanted to rip them apart, limb from limb. But the more you spoke, the more the words lingered inside my head, and I began to see what you were saying. Good job."

"Yeah, it surprised all of us, I think," Miri said.

"Well, with that said, I wanted to say thank you, and I'm sorry I seemed so...cold toward you earlier."

"No need to apologize. Your brother explained it all," I said.

"By the way," Malfae said as she started to walk away. "I want you both to join the Ranger Brigade. You don't have to answer now, but sleep on it. I'll get back with you tomorrow. You can have your answer then, but just know I will not take no for an answer." Malfae lifted her hood overhead and disappeared into the crowd scattered around the kingdom.

"Oh, how exciting, us as part of the Ranger Bri—"

"Almost scary if you think about it," I interrupted Miri. "Me, a Ranger? You know how clumsy and anxious I am. I mean, sure, I did well tonight, but who knows what'll happen next."

"Well," Kyna snuck up behind us, "What a great night, in a way, don't you think?"

"The ending was great. But people still died, Kyna."

"Yeah, that's true." Kyna hung her head. "But I think everyone learned something from it. And..." Kyna paused awkwardly for a moment. It was as if she were cheery, and Kyna never acts cheery. "Malfae wants all of us to join the Ranger Brigade!" Kyna said with excitement on her face. I had never seen her this chipper before. It was nice witnessing a friend with joy.

The thought of joining the Ranger Brigade was exciting. Only, I hadn't the slightest idea how to be a soldier or what it truly meant to be part of the Ranger Brigade. What type of training would we go through? What would our schedule be like? What responsibilities and duties would be involved? Sure, the war we just endured ended surprisingly well; we welcomed the pack to join Zynthia as one people. Despite the loss on both sides, that was a win in my book. Still, my skills as a warrior and knowledge of the strategies involved with battle were little to none. Had it not been for the light that is inside me, would we have prevailed? Would I, or my friends, be dead? And what about the others? Besides Kyna, no one in the group seemed too enthused about the idea. On the other hand, we would get to live in Eru Psyawla, a prosperous city streaming with beauty and the lively spirits of the people, or at least it was. Something to think about, I suppose. Miri walked up and kissed me on the cheek.

"Thinking about the Ranger gig, huh? I know, it's exciting but also scary at the same time. I think we should do it."

"Now, how did you know what I was thinking?"

"That look on your face when you're deep in thought or confused," Miri said. I sat next to Miri, daydreaming of us training together as Rangers, living in Eru Psyawla, and possibly being married someday, and a smile sprung to my face.

"What's that smirk for?" Miri chuckled while pushing her shoulder into mine.

"Just thinking what it might be like to live here, and I think you're right. We should take Malfae's offer, all of us." Miri smiled and laid her head on my shoulder, placing her hand in mine.

"I know."

We swept through debris and ash through the morning and into the afternoon. We may have ended on a high note, but going through everything that was lost put a sour taste in my mouth. It was hard to believe something like this could happen in a place like Zynthia. Thankfully, Jordiah and his pack were pitching in on a good chunk of the mess, thanks to his newfound peace with the kingdom. I know they say I had everything to do with ending the feud and hatred he had for this place, but part of me knew he had it inside of him all along, behind all the anger and sadness. It felt good cleaning up with Jordiah and his pack, getting to know them, and working together to right the wrong that we all had a part in.

"You know, Torren," Jordiah said. "Having a cousin could be like having a brother, if you think about it."

"I guess that's true, in some way, shape, or form. I'm just happy that we settled this thing, without any more harm or bloodshed," I replied.

"Yeah, but man, do we love the smell." Jordiah smiled as we pulled a slab of wood over to a burn pile. "I'm kidding, I'm kidding." Jordiah chuckled and slapped me on my upper back.

We all took a short break to eat some lunch, a few of us napped instead. I looked over at Aevin, slumped down in a chair holding a sandwich in his hand, about to drop it as he snoozed away in the sun. It was comforting when the sunshine gleamed on your skin. It sort of warmed you like a blanket on chilly night. Miri noticed me chuckle as she ate her makian soup.

"What is it? What's so funny?"

I pointed over at Aevin, and immediately, soup shot out of Miri's mouth like an eruption as she began to laugh uncontrollably.

"I'm sorry, I'm sorry. It's not that funny. He just looks like a little rag doll lying there in that chair. And do you see the drool running down his mouth?"

I smiled at her laugh, like it was the prettiest sound I'd ever heard. It was like...angels singing, or at least birds singing. Neither of those really fit the situation, but it was amazing to hear her laugh.

"I must be slap happy. Come one, let's go rest." Miri pulled me to a nearby pile of hay, where we took a little slumber. It had been a long few days. We all needed sleep. We all needed healing. Eventually, everyone took a nap, even Jordiah.

We awoke to the sound of trumpets screaming in the late afternoon. "Hear ye, hear ye," shouted a messenger from the balcony overlooking the courtyard. Miri and I staggered our way to the front, still feeling drained from not having enough sleep. We met Lorcan and Keela and happened to notice Aevin fall out of his chair, in surprise, with his half-eaten sandwich lying on the ground.

"Here, let me help you," Beatrix said while giggling as she passed him. Once on his feet, Beatrix and Brittany held his hands and guided him in our direction.

"What's this about? I was having a good dream," Aevin said.

"I don't know. But we're about to find out. Look!" I said. "What's Jordiah doing up there?"

Jordiah, Ralcord, Bella, and Valmera stood on the balcony. Jordiah had a cheerful smile on his face, as did Bella, while they stood in silence next to the king and queen, all holding hands.

"Beneath the rubble and ash lay loved ones from both sides. Buried with sadness and guilt, among other feelings. But on top of that rubble and ash lay hope for better days brought to light with many thanks to Torren and his friends. The kingdom thanks you!"

I could feel the stare from everyone around me, looking at me with joy, but I didn't like the attention, so I sank further back into the crowd. I never wanted attention, good or bad. It always made me feel uncomfortable.

"This hope, this new day beginning, shall be of alliance with a former enemy." All four on the balcony raised their hands together as the crowd cheered and whistled. "Jordiah and his pack shall join our kingdom as fellow Zynthians, as neighbors, and as friends. We agreed that he will be a commanding officer of the Ranger Brigade, but of his own platoon. He will still follow the orders of the High Council, including the orders of Commander Malfae. Let us give the werewolves a warm welcome and celebrate this day! The cleanup shall commence the following day!" The crowd cheered louder and began to sing and dance.

"But where's all the festive food and such?" Cormac asked as the crowd dispersed.

Even though the kingdom was more or less in ruins, the people celebrated like the king ordered. It felt necessary in a way. Shining a bit of light on all the chaos and destruction. Loved ones still mourned their losses but dwelled on new beginnings. Beatrix and Brittany were in good spirits, dancing to the music provided by the royal bards. The tunes were pleasant, though some were on a sadder note to give a last goodbye to those we lost during the battle.

"So, want to dance?" Miri asked, and she slid in beside me like she slipped through mud.

"I believe the man is supposed to ask the woman," I said.

"Well, I knew you would never ask, so I decided I would instead," she replied. I looked around and noticed all of our other friends dancing cheerfully, and I noticed the rubble around us. It made me not particularly in the mood for dancing and festivities.

"I don't, Mir. Maybe later." Without thought or warning, she grabbed my hands, dragged me to the dance floor, and began to sway, side to side.

"I'm not much of a dancer, Miri. What if I step on your feet?"

"Torren, does it look like I'm a good dancer? Just come here." She pulled me close to her, and we both began swaying in rhythm, perfectly dancing together. It was a slow dance, so it wasn't that hard, but still, the fact that I found a rhythm at all was miraculous enough.

"See, you're getting it," Miri giggled.

"I suppose I am."

After a few songs and a group sing-along, the party slightly died down a bit. Some of the songs of the werewolves' choice were rather...disturbing, but overall fitting, one could say. I found it to be a bit more fun than I imagined. The focus was on the kingdom as a whole, not just me or my friends, or Jordiah. I couldn't help but look at the twinkle in Miri's eye once we sat down to rest from all the dancing. It was magical in a way. It brought peace that, even though the sun was setting and the night awakening, the smallest light from her eyes could shine bright enough to illuminate the whole place. It was beautiful. She is beautiful. Her smile, her hair, her laughter. All the things that make her Miri are simply the best things in the world.

"What are you staring at? Do I have something in my teeth?" She tried using a piece of straw to pluck between her teeth.

"No, no, silly. Nothing's in your teeth," I said. "I just—I wanted to ask you something." I cleared my throat and let out a nervous sigh. "Miri, would you do me the hono—"

"Hey, guys, how are you enjoying the party?" It was Jordiah and Bella interrupting.

"Oh, hey. It's...fun," I replied. "Could use a little more mixberry bread, though."

"Yeah, first time I've had it, and I got to tell you, I'm not a fan," Bella said.

"You're nuts! It's only the greatest bread ever made," Miri argued.

"I mean, it's not terrible, it's just too sweet."

"Ladies, ladies. Calm down. It's only bread. Hey, Torren, Miri, how about me, you two, and Bella join up for a game of Stones and Sticks? Boys vs girls? Couple vs couple?"

"Wait, no one said Miri and I were a couple, per se." I could see the fire ignite in Miri's eyes as soon as I said it. "Okay, yes, we are a couple. Miri, what do you think?"

"I don't know, Torren. What do I think?" Miri slammed her hand down on the table and stared into my eyes like she was digging for my soul. "I'm just playing. Yes, we will play. Boys vs girls!"

The girls killed us at Stones and Sticks, even with Jordiah's natural talent for the game. His reflexes were some of the best I'd ever seen, and we still lost. "Better luck next time," Miri joked. It was nice being in that moment with Jordiah and Bella. It gave me and Miri a chance to see the gentle side of both of them. Behind the fur and fangs, they really were great people. Loyal to a fault, that's for sure.

"You know, I think I'm excited to have a cousin. Almost like having a brother, you think?"

"Yeah. I suppose so," Miri said. "Bella's pretty awesome to be around, fun, corky, little bit of spice but not too much."

"That's true. She is a little...yeah, spice is it. That's how I'd describe her," I agreed.

We circled the grounds searching for the rest of our friends, finding them near a tower playing...Shadow Hunter. Miri and I joined in on the game, and instead of using a lantern, I just used my palm. It was safer and easier than carrying around a lantern with an open flame. Needless to say, my gift didn't help me win much. I still lost, like usual, but it was okay. Playing two different games with two separate groups of people, one of them being former enemies, was a good night. We seemed to forget about the previous day and the events that occurred for a while, which was a bonus on top of the celebration. It was what the celebration was meant to do: help us grieve but move on and enjoy the things happening now. The games and the music lasted the majority of the night. Some people kept the festival alive all night long, hoping not to have to let it stop. I understood that because when the celebration ended, it meant dealing with ash and painful memories lying on the ground. But that was okay. Because in order for us to move forward, we had to take in those events and deal with them in the right way, with the right help.

Me and my friends, all seven of us laid silently under the stars once the celebration had died down. Jordiah and his pack had migrated to a separate field for the night but made sure we knew they were still near the castle as they let out cheerful howls and laughter as they slowly drifted to sleep.

"Thank goodness that's over with," I muttered.

"What are you talking about?" The celebration? It was wonderful," Keela said as she looked over at Lorcan, clearly love-stricken.

"Yes, I know. I know. Talking about the celebration, it was magnificent. I don't think I've played as many games or danced so much in my life. And I'm not good at either of those things," I replied. "I was talking about all the howling and noise coming from the wolves. They're animals, no pun intended. They're simply different. And while that's good in its own way, it's midnight, and they're yelling and causing a ruckus all over the kingdom. It's no wonder any of us can't sleep," I stated. "I mean that all with love."

"Well, we all have to get used to them. Besides, I don't think they smell all that bad either," Kyna said.

"Okay, now that is a lie, and you know it, just like we all do," Cormac said. In reality, yes, they did have a certain stench that could catch you by surprise, but in its special own little way, it was…nice.

"It's not terrible, I suppose," I said. "Just like we all have a certain scent that we give off."

Everyone else fell asleep rather quickly after our little conversation. I, on the other hand, couldn't sleep. My mind was drifting back and forth through memories of my mother and father. How I thought that one day they would meet my children and wrap them with sweets and warm hugs. I thought about how my children would never get to learn how their grandmother, Ailbhe, hand-crafted gifts for days on end, splinter after splinter, until it was just right and to her liking. Would they have a nickname for them? Like…Grandmother A, Ail, Bhe? Or what about Grandpa Ci for my dad? Hmmm. I'll let them decide once they're old enough, I suppose. As the thoughts ran through my head, I saw a shooting star stream across the sky. The child in me wanted to wake everyone around to see its beauty. The grown elf in me fought against it and won. I decided to let them sleep. They needed it. Tomorrow was designated for cleaning up, and it wouldn't be just physically exhausting; it would be emotionally and mentally taxing, too. Going through the rubble in which so many lives were lost, the bloodshed and tears that followed its path. The entire kingdom was drained, broken to the core over the events that occurred in the past few days. We didn't know how we would recover, but it started with the celebration. And no matter how much I picked at Jordiah and his pack, they knew I wanted them to be a part of this kingdom.

The next morning, the whole kingdom, including the werewolves, came together to clean up. It was amazing to witness the teamwork, the trust that everyone had for one another, even after everything that had happened such a short time before. Part of me had a feeling that Jordiah had some master plan for taking over the kingdom after winning everyone's trust. The other part of me saw what kind of person Jordiah really was and had to have faith in him, in his pack. They seemed to really enjoy being around everyone in Zynthia. Which was weird in a way because, just the other night, they were running around ripping people apart and destroying homes. I guess deep down, they really didn't want to be in a war. They just wanted a place to call home.

"Why don't you make yourself useful and come help me with this stack?" Jordiah asked. I couldn't help but notice something different about him as we walked closer.

"Okay. Yeah. We'll help." Me, Miri, and Kyna helped Jordiah clear debris of a burned-down house and realized his eyes had changed from a red-purple color to just purple.

"Hey, your eyes—they changed color. Did you know they could do that?"

"I hadn't noticed," Jordiah replied while picking up wood and moving it to a burn pile. "I guess we'll use this for the next festival, huh?"

"Either that, or we will use it to rebuild. Either way, it'll go to good use," I said.

"So, how did you escape from Tenebrae, anyway?"

"Torren, there are many things you still need to learn, some of which should never be used but known about. As you could see from my...ill-mannered actions, they lead to a darkened heart and bloodshed. Later on, I'll teach you what I learned from my mother's journal, if you like."

"I'll think on it. I'm not sure I want to know everything."

The sun had only been shining for a short while, but already we could feel its warmth blanketing us. It felt like it hadn't rained in days, and crops were in need of a fresh drink, so I grabbed some water cans and handed some to Aevin.

"Here. Help me give them some water. We'll need this crop pretty soon, and it's not looking too good." He nodded and helped me water the produce. While watering the plants, my mind slipped back to my parents. How when I was young we would go out to the garden, pulling weeds and tilling the soil every year. The way my father taught me to care for each plant to help it reach its full potential, my mom humming tunes while she so peacefully picked fresh beans and berries. Those were good days. Suddenly, a heart-gripping feeling tightened in my chest.

"Stop. Come with me."

"Wa—Wh—okay. I'm coming." Aevin and I dropped the watering cans and walked over to Miri. I looked over at Aurora and noticed she was acting skittish, scared even, like never before. She was jumping back on her hind legs and kicking. I looked up to the sky and held tightly to Miri's hand. Just over the horizon flew three terrifyingly angry dragons barreling toward the kingdom.

I looked at Miri and said, "I love you," as their roars echoed across the sky.

The end...

Milton Keynes UK
Ingram Content Group UK Ltd.
UKHW021418291124
3267UKWH00026B/105

9 798893 333237